SPLENDID LIGHT

A novel by

A. A. Akibibi

A. A. Akibibi

ISBN: 979-8-9856812-4-6
979-8-9856812-5-3

ACKNOWLEDGEMENTS

My sincere thanks to Isabel Lieb, who took my simple cover-design ideas and turned them into something incredible. Many thanks to my sister G.K., for her patience and generosity in helping me navigate the self-publishing world. And a tremendous thanks to you, the readers who have lived this adventure with Sean.

Yuayua Publishing
Le Center, MN

CONTENTS

A. A. Akibibi

CHAPTER 1

Splendid Light

Blinding light. Everything is too bright. It overwhelms my eyes, drilling into my mind like a plasma torch. I squint, trying to drive the painful dazzle away. I can't see anything. My surroundings are a uniform white blur. The atmosphere seems to sizzle, almost as if the air itself is about to catch fire. I remember descriptions of Jesus and Heaven from my pastor at church. Does this mean I'm going to see Mom?

As I scan around me, there is one area that isn't blindingly white. It takes me a moment to realize it's Johnson. His dark skin and dark clothes bring a hint of relief to my dazzled eyes.

A sudden loud, deep croak breaks the silence. My heart thuds at the unexpected noise. It sounds like the bullfrogs I used to hear down by the river in Victoria. But there aren't any bullfrogs on the bridge of the *Aurora*. The nearest one must be trillions of miles away, in another universe.

I pause, and concentrate on the sound. It takes my brain a second to recognize it as human speech, and another second for it to interpret the words, "What's happening?"

The truth hits me like a flaming meteor: we are back in our own space! Light has returned to normal. Our voices have returned to normal. No more squeaky chipmunks. This means I will get to see Bo and Hoss again, and eat pizza. I can't wait to eat a great, big, hot fudge sundae smothered in whipped cream! Just seeing the normal light, and hearing normal voices, makes me feel back at home. Everything is okay again.

"We made it," I hear someone else say. His voice is also very deep, like an answering bullfrog. My ears have grown used to hearing high-pitched squeals; our normal voices sound weird.

"Of course we made it!" a voice says brusquely. This would be the captain. "We need to find out where we are. Johnson, get us a reading!"

"Sir, my eyes need some time to adjust back to this light," the first officer replies. "I recommend we have the computer make the first check."

"Very well," the captain barks. "Computer, scan the stars and determine our location!"

"The scans are inconclusive," the computer replies right away. "No star clusters match any current charts, and no stars in scanning range match known stellar bodies."

"What the devil!" the captain blurts. "Keep scanning! Let me know the instant you find a charted reference point!"

Some of my excitement vanishes. I now realize we aren't home yet. We must be hundreds, if not thousands, of light years away from Earth if the computer doesn't recognize any of the stars, or even any cluster of stars. Which direction should we travel? How long will such a journey take?

The bridge, which only held the captain, Johnson, and Waph when I arrived, is filling up fast. Everything looks washed out; each new arrival strides through the hatchway looking like the white silhouette of a ghost. I hear a low rumble, like the voice of a bull elephant. That has got to be Wiggs chugging in.

The volume of noise has likewise increased dramatically – questions about what is happening, updates on our quandary, and suggestions for different ways to scan all mix together in a confusion of sound. My head is starting to spin, which doesn't help the pounding headache I have from the bright glare. How long were we in the space with the rainbow-colored light? I celebrated two birthdays there. It was definitely more than a year. My eyes have grown accustomed to seeing in the rainbow-colored light. Hopefully they can readjust quickly to normal light!

"Marcum to the bridge," I hear the captain bark.

There is a quiet pause, as if the *Aurora* itself is holding its breath. Then a low, slightly distorted voice answers, "Yes, sir."

This is further proof that we are back in our own space. Our communication equipment didn't function before. Now it appears to be working normally.

The bridge is getting crowded. My headache is getting worse. I need a quiet place where I can rest my eyes. Pushing my way past two of the scientists, I leave the bridge. It's a quick walk to the lounge. The lights are off in here, bringing a welcome relief to my eyes.

I gaze out the porthole, relishing the sight. There are no more rainbow-colored ribbons. The stars are now white pinpricks in a vast black sea. This is the way space is supposed to be.

Even so, the rainbow universe did have some positives. I enjoyed meeting the tulip people and sloth-bears. Sleeping in the reverse-gravity was great. I'm glad I've had the experience. If our rations weren't spoiling, and if our iridium didn't get used up so quickly, I wouldn't mind exploring it a bit more – as long as I knew we could get back.

I choose a couch and settle down. How long will it take us to reach Earth? Since we are low on supplies, surely we'll cut our mission short and go straight back home. That will give me a chance to tell Mr. D all about our adventures. I doubt he'll believe any of it. Who would possibly imagine that such a place exists?

My thoughts turn to the scientists. Who will be the one to guide us back? I'm guessing it will be Kartak. The crooked-fingered scientist was made to explore.

And then, like an electric shock, I suddenly remember: Dad! He is still locked in the brig for trying to rescue me from quarantine. I've talked to the captain about it twice, but he refuses to release my dad. Perhaps now he might be more open to the possibility…

I immediately jump up and return to the bridge. Fortunately, they have dimmed the lights – my head is feeling better, and I want to keep it that way. Everyone is still discussing our situation. It doesn't sound like they've come up with any good ideas.

My eyes spot the captain, and I move in close so that he can hear me over the babble. "Captain Sharta," I say meekly, trying to think of the best approach.

"Yes, what is it?" he says, sounding distracted.

"I was thinking my dad's area of expertise could be of some use right now in determining where we are," I say, deciding this is the best angle to use with the captain.

The captain doesn't respond. Did he hear me? Is he ignoring me, or is he actually thinking the possibility over? I don't know whether to rephrase my statement or stay silent.

After almost a full minute, the captain says, "Sean, you must understand how important it is for everyone to follow the rules." Okay, he's lecturing. It's obvious he is going to deny my request. I barely pay attention as he continues, "We must have consequences for breaking them. However, it would be a good idea to have everyone's input on this. I suppose he has learned his lesson. I will go release him from the brig as soon as I've given Marcum his instructions."

It worked! I can't believe I was able to convince him!

Deciding it would be best to leave the bridge, so that none of the adults could accuse me of being a nuisance, I head for my quarters. As soon as the door slides open, I glance to my right. This has been my routine every day since discovering Rafiki's cocoon. The cocoon's sides are still smooth, with no evidence that he is ready to emerge. How much longer will I have to wait? What will he look like? And what will he think of this white light?

CHAPTER 2

Yates Vs. The World

I grab my graphic pad and sort through my school files. If we are going back to Earth soon, I need to catch up on my studies. It will be embarrassing if I'm too far behind the people I've studied with. That must be avoided. I select the math file and slip it into the pad. Just as I start to review what I read last time, there's a loud rap on the hatch.

"Come in," I shout, looking up to see who it is. The hatch slides open and Dad strides in, followed closely by Wiggs and Kartak.

"I'm free!" Dad says, a huge smile on his face. "It's good to get out. The brig was so dull!"

I look at his beaming face. He spent that time in the brig because of me. I went to the dark planet to get iridium. A creature ripped through my suit. The captain placed me and Kartak in quarantine, in case we had picked up some disease from the planet. My dad tried to free us, to rescue us from the boredom. Instead he got locked up, and had to endure days of boredom himself.

"Thanks for trying to help us out of quarantine," I say, trying to emphasize my appreciation with my eyes. "I'm sorry you had to spend so much time in the brig."

"Oh, don't worry about it," Dad says, waving his hand through the air as if he's pushing something away. "After all, what are dads for?"

I grin. It feels good to have a dad.

Wiggs comes over and tilts my graphic pad so that he can read it. "Math, huh? Well guys, Sean's busy studying. I guess we'll have to do this without him."

Kartak hangs his head, pretending to look dejected. "That's too bad," he says, shaking his head. "I guess it's just the three of us."

Something is definitely up. Their behavior is tickling my curiosity. From the looks on their faces, they know it's driving me crazy. And they're enjoying every second of it. "What are you going to do?" I ask, looking at each of their faces in turn, trying to hide my curiosity as much as possible. They still look washed-out, but I'm starting to make out some details: the way Kartak's nostrils flare, the individual strands of Wiggs's goatee, a twitch above my dad's right eye.

"Oh, nothing much," Kartak says in an offhand manner. I'm not buying his casual attitude for a second. I can see the crinkle in his eyes and the slight twitch of his lip. "We were thinking of celebrating your dad's release. Your dad was telling me he hasn't played Stratagem since he was a teenager. The three of us are going to play against each other, and since you are the only one on the *Aurora* with equipment, we're forced to invite you as well. But, seeing as you're so busy…" he lets the statement hang in the air, obviously relishing the moment.

"Stratagem?" I say, feeling as light as a leaf on the wind. It's hard to imagine adults wanting to play Stratagem, but all three of them look giddy with excitement as they crowd by the door. "That would be awesome! Should we play as teams, or should it be everyone for himself?"

"I think since there's four of us, teams would be best," Kartak replies, chuckling at my enthusiasm.

"How about me and Wiggs against you and Dad?" I suggest, jumping up from my bunk and tossing the graphic pad onto the desk. I start collecting my devices from their spots around the cabin.

"I was thinking more along the lines of Yates vs. the World," Kartak says.

I ponder this as I start to stuff the smaller devices into my duffel. Wiggs has a great deal of experience with various strategy games. On the other hand, he is a big target. It will be easy to hit him. And hear him. And smell him. Perhaps it would be better to have my dad as a partner.

"We don't have any suits, and I only have one monitor," I say, thinking through the problem. "We'll have to dial down the tension in the crossbow so we don't injure anyone. And we'll have to modify a few graphic pads and tie them into the devices, so they can track when someone gets hit. It won't be perfect, but I think we can make it work."

Each of the adults has a graphic pad with him. Kartak helps me with the modifications to the pads. I make the adjustment to the crossbow, and then we're ready to set out.

I still can't believe they want to play Stratagem. As we walk, I steal glances at them. Will they be any good? Kartak will probably be a tough opponent. But Wiggs? With my skill we should dominate, even if Dad isn't very good.

We reach the elevator. I can feel the pulse in my neck. My senses are alert to every whisper, every faint scent, and every moving shadow around me. I still can't see completely clearly in the white light, but colors are starting to brighten, and objects are becoming more distinct. My eyesight should definitely be an advantage in this game.

The lift stops and the doors open. Kartak leads us to a hold. There is a maze of crates inside – plenty of places to hide. I heft the duffle from my shoulder and set it on the deck. Wiggs and Dad place the robots next to it. Kartak does the same with the crossbow and repeater.

"How are we going to do this?" I ask. "We don't have anyone to hide the devices around the hold."

"I figured we could just divide them up between the teams," Kartak replies.

"That's what I'm thinking," I say. "But how shall we divide them? Should we split them up together, or should the teams take turns choosing?"

"I think we should take turns choosing," Dad says. "That way, each team gets the devices they want."

"The only problem with that method is that Wiggs and I don't know all the devices," Kartak points out. "If Sean would be kind enough to give us a rundown on how they work, I think choosing them would be the best method."

I nod and empty the duffel, arranging the devices on the deck. After everything is laid out, I start explaining how each device works. I can tell the adults are impressed. Kartak seems especially intrigued by the occluder.

"And this laser fits over your hand and wrist like a gauntlet," I say, indicating the last device. "It's supposed to fit almost any size hand. You sight down your arm, and fire."

"Where's the trigger?" Wiggs asks, inspecting the device.

"There isn't a trigger," I explain. "To shoot, you squeeze your hand into a fist and hold it for a second."

Wiggs loosens the straps and tries it on. "It's a snug fit, but it works," he says, aiming at me. "I like it!"

"You guys can choose first," I say. Kartak nods. He and Wiggs start discussing their choice.

It takes much longer than I expect for all of the devices to be chosen. Wiggs and Kartak take their time, and even Dad drags the process out. He doesn't just accept my recommendations. He insists on debating every choice. Finally, we are ready to play.

Dad and I slip to the left when we enter the hold. Wiggs and Kartak go right. I slide between two rows of crates. Reaching an intersecting pathway, I glance right and catch a glimpse of Kartak, just before he disappears behind a stack of crates. I turn left and then take the next right. Dad has followed on my heels. I tilt my head to the right, indicating he should make his way back toward the hold entrance. I head the other way.

Two minutes later, the computer announces, "The game is starting in three, two, one."

I have found a spot between three stacks of crates and the back wall. It is a tight squeeze – none of the others could fit in here, and I'm hoping they don't realize I can. As an added bonus, there is a slight gap between two stacks of crates; it's just big enough for me to peer through. I'm glad Dad caved and let me take the repeater. This is a great spot for sniping opponents.

A slight ping catches my ear. Someone is just a yard or two down the nearest alley between crates. Is it my dad or one of the others? I hear the sound again. My mind filters through the different devices, trying to determine what I might be hearing. Could Wiggs be using a support beam to steady the laser? I strain my ears, but don't hear his heavy breathing. It must be either my dad or Kartak.

A shadow crosses the gap between the crates. I ease back until only a sliver of my eyeball is peeking through my spyhole, and hold my breath.

No figure comes into view. The person has stopped just short of the gap. It's Kartak. I just know it. And he suspects I'm back here. I don't know where my certainty comes from, but I'm confident it's true.

What will he do? What device can he use to trap me and take me out of the game? I shouldn't have hidden here, boxed in with no escape route. That's a rookie mistake!

After several tense heartbeats, I see a figure pass in front of my spyhole. It takes less than a second for my brain to recognize him. It's my dad. Some of the tension drains from my muscles. I let out my breath. I give my dad a few seconds to get farther down the alley, and then peek around the end box. It's time for me to get out of here. But first I have to make sure no one is lurking out there, waiting to pounce.

I wiggle between a stack of crates and the wall, wincing at the noise I'm making. It isn't loud, but it's enough to betray my position. Finally, I'm out of the hiding spot. I peek both ways down the alley. There isn't any movement, or any other hint that an opponent is nearby. I creep into the alley, heading to the right. Reaching an intersection, I pause and take a breath. There is no sound. I glance back to make sure no one is sneaking up from behind. Then slowly, very slowly, I crouch down low and ease forward, careful not to brush up against the crates next to me.

I peek around the corner. The huge figure of Wiggs is about halfway down the aisle, creeping away from me. I slowly ease the repeater up into position. Wiggs is centered in my sight. I fire a quick burst and duck back, smiling. I doubt he has any idea where the hits came from.

Glancing around to make sure my alley is still clear, I creep slowly back the way I came. At the next intersection, I check to make sure it's empty, and sneak around the corner. After taking a few careful steps, a slight noise makes me pause. Which direction did it come from? I slowly rotate around, searching high and low for an attacker.

A terrible bang makes me jump. My heart starts pounding in my chest. I gaze around, wondering what could possibly have made the noise.

"That sounded like an explosion!" Kartak says, appearing from behind a stack of crates to my right. He sprints from the room. I rush after him, dodging around Wiggs, who is chugging toward the door as fast as he can go.

As I exit the hold, I hear the sound of pumps thumping furiously. Kartak is inspecting the water tanks. A moment later, he takes off for the elevator. I slide in with him, wondering what we will find on the upper level. Is the hull breached? Should we be wearing spacesuits?

We exit the lift, and Kartak immediately turns right. He seems to have an idea what's going on. I follow close on his heels as he jogs around the wishbone junction into the port corridor.

Marcum is sprinting toward us from the opposite end of the hallway. He skids to a halt in front of the new hydroponics room. The *Aurora's* engineer hits the hatch sensor and then leaps back with a startled yelp. A rush of water chases after him, hits the far wall, and starts heading both ways down the corridor. I barely avoid crashing into Kartak from behind as he slams to a halt.

"Must be a burst pipe!" Kartak shouts, over the sound of gushing liquid. "We have to get it turned off before we lose all of our water." He charges ahead, wading through the ankle-deep flow.

I hesitate a moment, wondering what I should do. Deciding it's possible I could be of some help, I step into the rushing water. It's cold. Soon my shoes and ankles are soaked. Ignoring the discomfort, I forge ahead and turn into the hydroponics room.

Water is gushing from a pipe in the back of the room. Kartak and Marcum reach the area and immediately get to work. The slosh of water tells me other adults have arrived. Wiggs appears on my left, the captain passes me on the right, followed closely by Johnson. Tension is heavy in the air. Our survival depends on getting the water stopped, and soon.

Johnson joins Kartak and Marcum. As they work, a thought pops into my mind. "Isn't there an automatic cutoff?" I say, to no one in particular.

"Normally there is," Wiggs replies, finally catching his breath. "But these vats were cobbled together out of whatever parts we could find. There are spare valves for the main hydroponics bay. Unfortunately, in the rush to get these vats finished, they must have been overlooked."

I glance up. There is a look of anguish on his face. He is blaming himself for this situation.

"Nobody is to blame for this," I say, trying to boost his mood. "Don't worry, Kartak will have it sorted out soon."

"Sean, I could use your help over here," Kartak says in a strained voice.

I immediately splash through the water to where he is wrestling with a wrench. "I need you to fit this in there," he says, indicating a metal ring sitting on a vat to his left. Nodding, I lift the ring, and follow his instructions on where to place it.

We work for what seems like hours. I'm amazed that the storage tanks haven't run dry long ago. At long last, the flow of water thins to a trickle, and then cuts off completely. Marcum gives a satisfied grunt. "That should do it." Turning a sweaty face to Johnson, he says, "We need to recover as much of the water as possible."

"Waph has been working on that," Johnson replies. "I'll go see how it's coming along."

I straighten up. The stooped position I was working in has left my back sore. My clothes are soaked through, I'm shivering from the chill water, and I'm exhausted. I need to change. After that, a bit of a nap would be good.

Kartak slaps me on the back. "Thanks for your help, Sean," he says wearily. "I need to go down to the pump room and make sure everything is functioning properly. Why don't you get some rest."

I nod. "Good luck," I say, hoping that everything is now back in working order. After nodding to Wiggs, I head out the hatch. My shoes squelch and water oozes out of the carpet with each step I take. I reach my cabin, and the hatch slides open.

Despite my weariness, my mind is tickled by the fact that something isn't right. I pause just inside the doorway and look around. My eyes land on Rafiki's cocoon – or what's left of it. The cocoon has been shredded, with tatters hanging limply to the left and right.

A growl comes from my left. My head whips around, I spot Rafiki, and my insides seem to freeze. No, it can't be!

I'm staring into the eyes of a strong-jaw.

CHAPTER 3

Rafiki

They are no longer the large, liquid eyes of my friend. They are the cold eyes of a killer. And he is staring straight at me. A second snarling growl and a flashing movement seem to shake me from my stupor. I jump back into the corridor and slap the hatch sensor.

There is a loud thud as Rafiki hits the closing hatch. Snarling and snapping, he lunges at me. I watch, horrified, as he forces his muzzle into the opening.

The door reverses direction.

In a second or two, the gap will be wide enough for him to squeeze through. I slap the sensor over and over again in a panic. The door starts to slide shut, but I know it won't close all the way.

I take off sprinting down the corridor. A series of frenetic scratching sounds, followed by heavy footfalls, warns me that Rafiki is free. Knowing he must be catching up, I dodge to the left. Rafiki's jaws snap shut where my right leg was a second before.

He stumbles for a moment, thrown off balance by the miss, but then lunges at me again. I hop away. Again he attacks, but I manage to sidestep it. Rafiki's lunges are clumsy. The white light must be confusing him. Or perhaps he is still getting used to his new body after the metamorphosis. That doesn't matter, though. I am out in the open. Rafiki will keep attacking me. One misstep is all it will take. And even the tiniest nip from him could prove fatal.

I angle toward the right side of the corridor and wait. Rafiki pounces again. I dodge out of the way, and watch as his head cracks against the wall. He is momentarily off-balance. Taking advantage of the opening, I resume my sprint down the corridor. All-too-soon, the sound of his pounding paws fills my ears. Looking over my shoulder, I see Rafiki gather himself.

There is no cover, no protection from his attack.

In desperation, I dive down to my left. A flash of movement catches my eye. Careful to stay as low as possible, I turn my head to look.

Rafiki is sailing over my head. His paws are thrashing wildly, trying to change his momentum mid-air, trying to reach me. He thuds to the deck a couple of yards past me, and slides another yard or so.

I'm trapped. My doom is staring me in the eyes. Soon Rafiki will be able to reverse his momentum and renew his attack. He will wear me down until I make a mistake.

I gaze around frantically, trying to spot anything I can use as a weapon. And realize that the open hatch of the lounge is inches from my hand.

I scramble up, just as Rafiki regains his balance, and dash through the doorway. The instant I'm clear, I slap the hatch sensor. Rafiki is charging, the light of madness in his eyes. The hatch is sliding shut, but too slowly. Rafiki will wedge his muzzle in the doorway again, and the hatch will reverse, opening the way to his prey. He is snarling and spitting. The sound sends shivers up my spine. Surely this can't be the same creature I used to snuggle close to my chest, or feel purring against my cheek.

The hatch is still open about eight inches. I stare into Rafiki's cold, pitiless, killer eyes, see his slavering fangs, feel the blast of his hot breath. Any moment now, the hatch will start sliding open again…

Rafiki lunges. His muzzle hits the frame of the hatch. But the white light has betrayed him. He is angled wrong. Instead of coming straight for the gap between the hatch and the frame, he has hit the outside edge of the frame. The hatch clicks shut on his guttural growls. My hand is instantly on the sensor plate, locking the hatch so that something doesn't accidentally trigger it open.

I stand for a moment, panting. My brain seems to be working in slow motion. I can't figure out what to do. I'm safe for now, but... but I have to warn the others. And the best person to start with would be... "Computer, where is Kartak?" I ask, my voice a dry croak.

"Kartak is checking the water storage tanks," the computer replies.

That's right. I had forgotten he was going down to the lower level. Most of the others are probably down there with him. That should give me some time.

I switch on the intercom by the hatch, and tap in the sequence for the water storage room. A few seconds later, a voice growls, "What is it?"

This isn't good. It's Sharden. I definitely don't want to talk to him. "I need to speak with Kartak."

"He's busy," Sharden says tersely.

"I need to speak with him *now*," I say firmly, fighting down a surge of panic. What if Sharden remains stubborn?

There is silence. It stretches out for several heartbeats. "Are you still there?" I ask, wondering if Sharden has decided to just ignore me.

More silence. What should I do?

Then, "I'm here, Sean." This time it is Kartak's voice.

"Kartak, listen," I say, speaking quickly. "Rafiki is out of his cocoon –"

"That's great news, Sean!" Kartak says.

"And he's a strong-jaw," I finish with a rush, feeling the sting of betrayal. Rafiki was my friend. Now he wants to kill me.

There are several seconds of silence. Then Kartak says, "Could you repeat that?"

He isn't sure he heard me correctly. Or perhaps he doesn't want to believe what he heard. "Rafiki is a strong-jaw, and he got out of my cabin before I could get the door shut."

"Are you hurt?" Kartak asks, sounding concerned. "Did he get you at all?"

"No," I reply. "The white light seems to confuse him. I was able to dodge his attacks."

"Did you lock the door to the lounge?" Kartak asks. He can obviously see that I'm in the lounge from the screen on the intercom.

"Yes, it's locked. Is everyone else with you?" I ask, and hold my breath.

"A couple of people. Everyone else should be on the bridge," he replies. "I'll let them know the situation, and then Sharden and I will do some hunting. Just stay where you are for now."

I nod, and then realize he can't see me. "Understood," I say. The intercom screen goes dark. Now comes the waiting.

I sit on the edge of a couch, and jump right back up and start pacing. Is everyone else truly on the bridge? What if someone is wandering around? And is the bridge hatch closed? If Rafiki gets there before Kartak can warn them, and if the bridge hatch is open…

My mind replays images of Roberts after he was attacked by strong-jaws. Being as gentle as possible as we secured him to a bunk of the lander, to minimize the pain from the deep rips in the skin of his back. The sight of Roberts, when we thought he was healthy again and he was about to be released from sickbay. And then he was dead. How many people will Rafiki tear up with his teeth and claws today? How many people will die because I brought him on board? Rafiki seemed so cute and cuddly, and he was dying of cold. I saved him. How could things have turned out so horribly?

I realize that this is the true danger of encountering unknown aliens. Even if the species is intelligent, and seems to be working cooperatively with you, a single difference in customs, or one slight miscommunication, and the situation could turn lethal. You can never be absolutely certain you understand the way they think or feel. Heck, I often don't understand how other humans think or feel! I now understand how very dangerous every strange environment we visit, or unknown life form we encounter, can be.

My clothes still cling to my body. As the intensity of Rafiki's attack fades a bit, I become more aware of how cold I am. My body starts to shiver. I walk faster, and rub my hands along my arms, trying to warm up.

The day seems to drag on. It's horrible, not knowing what the situation is. I want to take a peek into the corridor, but this could get me killed. It's my own fault I'm in this situation. I just have to bear it.

My legs start to burn from all my pacing. My clothes are mostly dry, and although there is still a bit of chill to the air, I'm no longer shivering. I settle on a couch in the front row and stare out the porthole. Stars are streaming past. Each one of them is an unknown. No human has ever explored their systems, or possibly even set eyes on them. I could be the first person to see each one.

"Sean?" The voice from the intercom makes me jump. I'm instantly on my feet, racing around the couches.

"I'm here," I say, my heart driving against my ribcage. What will the news be? How many people are injured? How many are dead?

"We got him," Kartak says.

"Did anybody…" I can't finish the sentence. My throat is too tight.

"We were able to warn them in time," Kartak says, evidently anticipating my question. "Nobody is hurt."

My chest loosens a bit at the news. Everyone is safe.

"Thanks," I say, leaning against the wall to steady myself. "For everything."

"You're welcome," Kartak replies. The intercom screen changes. Kartak has turned it off at his end.

I stand still for almost a full minute, feeling my heartbeat gradually slow to a normal pace. Pushing off the wall, I stride over to the sensor pad and unlock the hatch. It slides open –

" –er get my hands on him, I'll wring his neck," the captain booms. He is facing away from me, but as soon as the hatch is fully open, he spins around. His eyes lock onto mine. They are flaming with fury. He starts striding toward me, a locomotive picking up steam. "Sean, you – "

"Captain, can I speak with you a moment?" Kartak says, loudly and firmly. He has just rounded the wishbone junction. He dodges around Sharden and Hollins, and hastens toward us.

The captain doesn't slow down. I want to run and hide from his anger, but I know it won't do any good. A few more steps and he'll be in arm's reach. "Captain!" Kartak says sharply.

The captain stops. "What is it?" he bellows over his shoulder, spit spraying the deck around him.

"I need to talk with you," Kartak says. "Alone."

How can he be so calm when the captain is about to erupt? And what could he possibly want to say to the captain right now? I wait nervously, watching the captain; his chest is heaving, his face is scarlet, and his hands are in front of him, as if he is actually preparing to wring my neck.

"It had better be quick!" the captain growls.

Kartak looks at me and gives a quick tilt of his head, indicating I should step out of the lounge. I hastily sidle into the corridor, keeping as far away from the captain as possible. The captain glares at me as he storms past into the lounge. Kartak quietly follows him. The door hisses shut.

"You're a dead one now," Sharden says gleefully.

"Shut up," I snarl, my heart racing once more. I was wrong to think that everyone is safe. With the captain this furious, I will be lucky to survive the day.

The seconds tick by. What could they possibly be talking about? Once more I feel the urge to disappear, but that would just make the captain even angrier – if that's even possible. Johnson, Marcum, and the rest of scientists appear at the end of the corridor. They join Sharden and Hollins.

"What's going on?" Johnson asks.

"The captain wants to skin Sean alive," Sharden says, a look of pure joy on his face. "Kartak has intervened. They're talking in the lounge."

Johnson looks like he's about to say something when the lounge hatch opens. The captain emerges. His eyes are glowering, but his face no longer has a ruby tinge. Apparently, Kartak has somehow managed to calm him down a bit. Even so I cringe, awaiting my doom.

"You will be confined to quarters for three days to contemplate what you've done," the captain says gruffly. "Meals will be brought to you. Your behavior could have cost the lives of everyone on this ship. I hope that truly sinks in. Because if you ever do anything this foolish again, I *will* space you."

"Yes sir," I say meekly, quite surprised my punishment isn't far worse. Kartak must truly have a magical gift of words.

Avoiding everyone's eyes, I quickly turn and walk to my cabin. I nearly got everyone killed. Now I must serve my sentence.

CHAPTER 4

Punishment

I'm locked in my cabin. Gazing around, I wonder how I will pass the time. My eyes land on the far corner, where the tatters of Rafiki's cocoon hang limply. In an instant I'm on my feet, ripping the coarse material from the wall. It's too much of a reminder of my friend. And of the peril in which I placed the ship. I have to clean it all off, to remove any evidence of the near catastrophe.

The cocoon material scrapes and cuts into my hands. I ignore the pain, tugging and twisting and tearing and scraping with my fingernails until I've removed every fiber of the cocoon. I jumble the shreds into a bag and slide it under the bed, hidden, so that I don't have to constantly look at the grim reminder of my mistake. When I'm released, I will chuck it into the incinerator, bag and all – I don't want to ever touch the stuff again.

Next I grab a rag, and scrub at the discoloration on the wall left by the cocoon. It doesn't help. The wall bears a stain that no amount of soap and water will remove.

Sighing, I toss the rag into a laundry bin in the bathroom and slump onto my bed. All of the adrenaline I felt during Rafiki's attack has drained away. My body is aching and weary. I lie back and close my eyes.

I am awakened by a pounding on the hatch. Sliding off the bed, I stumble groggily over and slap the sensor. It's Kartak, with a tray of food.

"I thought you might want something to eat," he says, and strides in. "And perhaps a little company. I can't stay long, or the captain will have a fit. But perhaps long enough for you to finish eating."

He sets the tray on my desk and settles onto the chair.

"Thanks," I mumble, not wanting to meet his eyes. I could have gotten him killed... I brush away the thought as I pick up a carrot. "Thanks for talking to the captain. I would probably be in the brig for the rest of the trip if it wasn't for you."

"It was a mistake anyone could make," Kartak replies. "Rafiki looked cute and cuddly to me. I never would have guessed he would transform into a strong-jaw."

"Yeah, sorry. I could have gotten you, me, and everyone else k—"

"That's enough, Sean," he cuts across me firmly. "Don't beat yourself up over it. You made a mistake, and it's over. You have to just let it go and move on."

"But –"

"No buts," Kartak says firmly. "Besides, after you and your dad managed to weasel your way out of losing to us in Stratagem, the hunt gave me the perfect opportunity to use my awesome tracking skills."

"Hey, I can't help that the pipe decided to burst in the middle of our game," I protest, though only half-heartedly. Kartak's teasing breaks through my gloomy mood and almost brings a smile to my face. "How did you get him?"

"The white light really seemed to confuse him," Kartak explains. "I spotted him prowling outside sickbay in the starboard corridor. He heard me arrive on the elevator. He was facing toward me, but gazing around as if he couldn't really see me.

"I quickly got him in my sights," Kartak continues, leaning back in his chair as he warms up to his story, "using a low-powered setting on the repeater in case I missed – I didn't want to accidentally damage some critical piece of equipment. The first several shots didn't appear to have any effect. I increased the power slightly, but it still didn't slow him down. When he sprang at me, I hit him in the muzzle with the butt of the repeater. That seemed to daze him. I fired several more bursts directly into his eye. After a few seconds, his muscles went slack. I wasn't taking any chances, though. Now that he was at point-blank range, I switched to full power and fired three quick bursts.

"Then I put on a pair of gloves and grabbed his hind legs – being very careful of his claws – while Sharden kept the repeater aimed at Rafiki's head. I dragged him into the elevator, we rode it down, and I dragged him to the airlock, watching carefully for any sign of life. It wasn't until we had sealed the airlock and sent him out into space that I truly relaxed. Now he's gone," Kartak finishes, his voice trailing off thoughtfully. Perhaps it's just my imagination, but I get the impression that the crooked-fingered scientist understands how I feel: about losing a friend; about the betrayal; about the fear of a deadly attack.

"Well, it looks like you're done," Kartak says, slapping his thighs and standing up. He collects my tray, turns toward me, and favors me with a lopsided grin. "I'll be here around eight. Aren't you lucky? You get breakfast in bed."

"Yeah, this is such a fantastic vacation," I say, returning his smile.

"I'd better skedaddle before the captain has my hide," he says, and bustles toward the hatch. "Take care!"

With that, Kartak hurries into the corridor. The hatch slides shut. I'm alone once more. Only now, things don't look so bad. I grab my graphic pad, flip to where I left off when Dad, Wiggs, and Kartak barged in to play Stratagem, and settle down to study.

Three days of studying, practicing alone with my Stratagem devices, and playing the simplistic games on my graphic pad. Three days without any news of events outside my cabin, except for little tidbits Kartak drops as he brings my food or picks up the tray (he is no longer allowed to stay and chat with me while I eat). My seclusion should be ending; but when?

Seventy-two hours have passed since I was locked up. Am I free to go? Or must I wait until tomorrow morning? How will I know when I can leave my cabin? I doubt the captain will come and tell me. Will he allow someone else to come set me free? I'm itching to leave; this has been worse than the quarantine after the dark planet – at least then, I had people to chat with. The problem is, if I set foot outside my cabin and the captain doesn't agree that my sentence is up, he could extend my confinement, or worse – throw me in the brig.

And if I convince the computer to ask the captain whether I've served my time, that would likely irritate him. I don't want to risk the possibility of being locked up even longer.

Ten minutes pass. Twenty. An hour. Nobody is coming to get me. I'm going to be alone for another evening. And what if someone doesn't come for me tomorrow? Should I dare to leave? Deciding to tackle that problem when it comes, I head into the bathroom. The knock comes just as I'm closing the door.

It takes me less than two seconds to reach the hatch sensor. The hatch swishes open. Wiggs is standing there, grinning.

"I thought you would be in more of a hurry to escape," he says, scratching his arm absent-mindedly.

"I wasn't sure my time was up, and I didn't want to emerge too early," I explain.

"Yeah, I suppose it would be best to play it on the safe side," Wiggs says, now stroking his goatee.

"What's been happening?" I ask, relishing the feeling of freedom I get as I step through the hatchway.

"We recovered as much of the water as possible," Wiggs replies, as we head down the corridor. "Roughly eighty percent of it. We also saved most of the plants, and made repairs to the vats. We now have a cutoff valve on the main pipe." He stops outside the lounge and gestures toward the hatch. "You are now banned from the bridge, so you will have to meet Sharden in there. He has some tasks for you to do." Wiggs shakes his head. "Sorry about that. Good luck!"

I watch numbly as he turns and heads for the wishbone junction. *Sharden* has tasks for me to do? I would rather go back to my confinement.

Knowing it would be useless to petition the captain for someone else to work with, I eye the hatch sensor. It's best to get this over with. Squaring my shoulders, I hit the sensor and enter the lounge.

"It's about time you showed up!" Sharden growls from just inside the door, making me jump. I thought he would be sitting on one of the couches, not standing so close to the hatch. "The captain sure was soft on you," he continues, glaring at me. "First we lose most of our water when a pipe bursts. A pipe *you* helped to set up. Then you release a killer animal onto the *Aurora*. I had to hunt it down and get it off this ship, nearly getting my arm ripped off in the process. How you avoided the brig is beyond me. You should have received thirty lashes and then been sealed up, never to see the light of day again. Yes, the captain was soft on you. Believe me, I won't be."

This leaves me speechless. He's saying the burst pipe was my fault, which it clearly wasn't. Plus, we recovered most of the water. And he makes it sound as if he single-handedly took care of Rafiki. He barely did anything. I doubt Rafiki ever got within pouncing distance of Sharden before Kartak took him down. The problem is, if I argue, it will only make things worse. I stand in the hatchway, trying to remain as calm as possible. When I feel confident I have control of my voice, I say, "Wiggs told me you have some tasks for me."

"That's right," Sharden says, smiling maliciously. "There is a bucket and a pile of rags in the utility room with your name on them. Once you pick them up, we'll get started."

Without a word, I turn and exit the lounge. As I stride down the corridor, I hear Sharden keeping pace behind me. I feel like a condemned criminal of the dark ages, heading for the execution block. It doesn't take me long to reach the utility room. As promised, there is a large bucket of cleaner and a pile of rags sitting in the middle of the floor. I pick them up and cock an eyebrow at Sharden.

"We'll start in sickbay," Sharden says, the glee evident in his voice and in the flashing of his eyes. After I lug the bucket down the corridor, Sharden waves me into the sickbay. My eyes quickly confirm that it's going to be just the two of us. Great.

"Start with the walls," Sharden says, pointing to the right of the hatch frame.

The work is tedious. Sharden keeps finding spots that I "missed". Soon my back is aching, my arm is aching, and my calves are sore. I try to ignore all the taunts and insults Sharden hurls at me, and concentrate on my dull task. Hours pass. When I have finally returned to my starting point, Sharden says, "And now for the deck."

I drop wearily to my knees and start swiping the rag across the deck. My entire body is aching now, but I don't stop. I just want to get this over with. I'm sure suppertime is long past, but Sharden doesn't allow me to stop. At last I reach the final few yards, and quickly wipe them down.

Done. I sit back on my heels and stretch out my back. Both of my arms are burning. There is a sharp pain in my knees. I wring the cloth into the bucket, and slowly rise to my feet.

"Good. Perfect timing," Sharden says gloatingly. "Supper should be cleared away. Get fresh cleanser in your bucket, and then you can clean the dining room."

I stand for a moment, wishing I misheard. I don't think I can clean another square yard, much less an entire room. But there's nothing I can do. The captain has put Sharden in charge of me, and Sharden won't let me off. This is my punishment for bringing a strong-jaw aboard. It's well-deserved. Even so, I won't give Sharden the satisfaction of hearing me complain. I'll show him that I can take whatever he dishes out.

Steeling my aching muscles, I hoist up the bucket and head for the utility room. I work as slowly as I can to dump the old cleanser and fill the bucket back up with fresh stuff. My muscles need as much of a break as I can give them before going back to scrubbing. Now the bucket is full and I have clean rags. I can't stall any longer.

I start with the table. The crumbs of food make my stomach rumble. Sharden must hear it – his smirk grows even bigger.

Next come the walls. And then the deck. My muscles are cramping up. Two-thirds of the floor remain. I'm not sure how much more of this I can take, but I push myself to keep going. Half a room left. My muscles are seizing up. I pour all of my focus into swiping a bit more of the deck. I can't give Sharden any excuse to make things harder on me than they already are.

Eventually, the room is spotless. I slump down, panting slightly, trying to ease my aching muscles.

"Hmm," Sharden says after "inspecting" my work. "I suppose it will have to do. You can be done for the day. Go get your bucket ready for tomorrow. I expect you in the utility room by seven o'clock." Throwing one final smug smirk at me, he turns and leaves.

I remain where I'm at, trying to will-away the pain and gather up some strength. It is several minutes before I can stand. The trip to the utility room is excruciating; my muscles feel as if they are tied into one giant knot. I somehow manage to dump the bucket and refill it. Tossing the dirty rags into the laundry bin, I shuffle to the kitchen.

There is very little to eat. I scrounge up a few strips of meat, half a bell pepper, and a small carrot. After that I head to bed. My aching muscles make it hard for me to get to sleep. And I dread waking up – no doubt I will face more of the same torture, only this time it will last all day.

When I arrive at the utility room at seven o'clock, Sharden confirms my suspicions. "We'll get started in the library."

After that it's hydroponics, and then the lounge. Today the work is even worse. My body started out sore, and now the pain leaves me on the verge of tears – it's that excruciating.

I work my way around the walls of the lounge, until I get back to the viewport. There is only the frame left. I glance out as I wipe it down. From this angle, I can see a bright point of light ahead of the *Aurora*. We are approaching a star.

"Keep working," Sharden says, heading toward the hatch. "When I get back, I expect to see a clean deck!"

The hatch swishes shut behind him. I assume he is going to lunch. My own stomach sounds like it has a lion living inside it. Would it be possible to sneak out and grab a snack without Sharden noticing? Probably not. I can't risk it.

Sighing, I sink to my knees and start on the deck. I weave my way through the rows of couches. They sit there, tantalizing me. A few minutes of relaxation would feel so tremendous right now. I decide that if I get finished before Sharden returns, I will grab a quick rest. After all, he hasn't given me my next assignment yet.

I reach the halfway point and pause to look out the viewport. The star doesn't appear to be any larger than before. I return to work, knowing Sharden might return at any second.

Finally! The last deck plate is sparkling. Setting my rag on the edge of the bucket, I gaze out the porthole to check our progress. This time, the star does seem bigger. Perhaps my eyes are deceiving me, but there also appears to be something else as well. Could it be a planet? Squinting doesn't help. I can't make it out.

My muscles are on fire. The lounge is dark and soothing. I flop down on the nearest couch and close my eyes.

When I open them again, it takes a while for the room to come into focus. My mind is a bit fuzzy. I have been sleeping. How long was I out?

I suddenly remember the star. Too sore to stand up, I roll off the couch and crawl to the porthole. At first, I don't see anything. The angle is different. It takes a bit of time, but after placing my cheek flat against the porthole, I finally spot the star. And there is definitely something out there along with it. It does appear to be a planet. From this distance, the orb is still barely larger than a grape. It will be a while before we are close enough to see anything.

The others must have discovered the planet as well. This is the only thing I can think of that would divert Sharden's attention away from my chores for so long. I'm certainly not going to complain. Feeling my stomach rumble, I find myself wondering if the planet will hold his attention for a while longer. I'm going to chance it. After all, I have to eat sometime.

I plod to the kitchen. There are a few leftover vegetables. I add these to a plate of meat slices, then sink wearily into a chair in the dining room. I nibble at the food, making the meal last as long as possible.

After finishing, I realize I still haven't taken Rafiki's cocoon to the incinerator. The corridor is empty when I exit the dining room; everyone must be on the bridge. This suits me. I retrieve the bag with the cocoon remains from my cabin and head to the incinerator. Once I arrive, I pause. This is the last reminder I have of my friend. I think about all of the fun we had together, and the way he would vibrate when snuggled up against me. No matter how he turned out in the end, I decide that I'm glad I rescued him.

A wave of heat blasts against my cheeks as I open the incinerator. It reminds me of Mom at the funeral home. I quickly dump the bag inside and seal it shut. Not wanting to stay here a moment longer, I shuffle to my room. It's time for another nap. If Sharden needs me, he can find me here. Weary from scrubbing walls and decks, it doesn't take long to fall asleep.

———

I wake up feeling a bit less fatigued. My cabin chrono says... no, it can't be. It's almost morning? I've slept for more than thirteen hours! No wonder I feel a bit refreshed.

There's plenty of time before my next work shift. Anxious to see our progress, I head to the lounge. My mind flashes back to the incinerator. Mixed thoughts of Mom and Rafiki run through my head. Hoping to distract myself from my mourning, I gaze out the viewport.

The planet has grown considerably. But this isn't what makes the breath catch in my throat. I stare stupidly at something in the lower-right corner of the porthole. Surely I must be mistaken. I squint, trying to strain my eyes to see farther. Time ticks by. We get closer. I can see it more clearly. There is no longer any doubt in my mind. This planet is unlike any we have visited so far.

I'm looking at a space station.

It is oddly shaped, and doesn't resemble any space station made by humans. But it is clearly not a naturally occurring object. It has been constructed.

Spotting movement off to the left, I turn and see an object moving away from the station. It banks around, and a sudden glow confirms my suspicions: it is a spacecraft, firing some kind of thrusters.

We have found other beings capable of space flight.

CHAPTER 5

New World

"We've tried monitoring and hailing the aliens on various frequencies. So far, nothing has worked." Wiggs picks up his tea and takes a sip. I sit forward, eager for any crumb of information I can obtain. All the action is on the bridge. Now that I'm banned, I have no idea what is going on. It's driving me crazy.

"At least they haven't made any hostile moves," Dad adds. "So far, they appear to be ignoring us."

"I find that strange," Wiggs says. "Unless their scanning equipment is immensely superior to ours, we are as unknown to them as they are to us. You would think they would try to communicate with us in some way."

"Maybe our ship is too small to be perceived as a threat," I point out, shifting around in my seat to get more comfortable. "Or maybe their minds are so alien, they don't experience fear and uncertainty the way we do."

"If their species has survived to the point that they've developed space travel, they must have *some* sense of danger, and how to counter it," Wiggs states firmly.

"I suppose you're right," I say, turning his statement over in my mind. "Still, they might react differently from us."

What are these aliens like? Will we be able to communicate with them? We need supplies. It's crucial that we make some kind of connection with the aliens.

The tulip people communicate using changes in color. The sloth-bears converse using a language that involves tapping. At first I hadn't realized they were trying to speak to us. Perhaps the aliens here *are* trying to communicate; we just haven't recognized it.

"Surely there must be other ways to try communicating," I say, racking my brain to come up with possibilities. The only ideas that seep out are the ones we've already tried. These keep crowding into my mind, preventing any new thoughts from forming. It's extremely annoying.

"Oh, we haven't given up trying," Dad assures me. "Next we're going to try the dhrychometer. I think it's a long shot, but Sharden feels it has a chance."

Sharden. The name makes the hair on the back of my neck prickle. I'm surprised he has time to make suggestions, considering he still spends most of his day monitoring my slave tasks.

Evidently, Wiggs interprets the look on my face. His eyes turn sympathetic as he says, "I know he works you hard, Sean, and that he can be more than a bit mean. But Sharden is a talented scientist. At this point, we're willing to try just about anything."

"Yeah, I know. That doesn't mean I have to like the source of the idea," I growl. Realizing my hand is gripping the edge of my seat tightly, I relax it, and recline back in my couch. "Look, I have to deal with him all day. I don't want to have to think about him at supper, too."

"Sure, what would you like to talk about instead?" Wiggs inquires.

"Well, there are those three space stations and all those ships," I say, gesturing toward the large viewport, "but I don't know anything about the planet." My eyes latch on to the globe we're orbiting, noting its colors and textures. "What's it like?"

"Those two land masses appear to be primarily savanna," Wiggs says, pointing with his left hand as he speaks. "However, on this large land mass there are several forests that, if our instruments are correct, are absolutely amazing."

"How so?" I ask, trying to picture the terrain in my head.

"Have you ever heard of a redwood?" Wiggs asks.

"I've seen a couple of holo-images," I reply.

"How about baobabs?" Wiggs inquires.

"I've seen a few on one of my field trips," I say, thinking back to the experience. It was my second time on the African continent. I was able to see many animals in their natural habitat, as well as a large variety of trees, including baobab and acacia. That had been one of my favorite weeks of school.

"Well," Wiggs says, sounding like the narrator of a nature show, "imagine a tree with the width-to-height ratio of a baobab, but that is much, much taller than a redwood." He smiles as he sees the dumbfounded look on my face. "Yes, that was my reaction as well."

"Imagine if you built a treehouse in one of those," Dad says. "You would be the envy of the neighborhood."

"Or if you had a body glider, you could jump from the top and glide to the ground," Wiggs says. "That would be quite the ride."

"I think I'll pass on that," I say, shuddering a bit at the thought. I have a fear of heights. If I tried jumping from that height, my heart might burst with fright.

I gaze at the splendor of the globe: tan and sage, blue and white, with some violet streaks near the terminator. A jagged mountain range splits one of the smaller continents in two down the middle. This is the first planet besides Earth that I have seen from space; truly seen, that is. The rainbow-colored light prevented me from seeing any details of the tulip people's planet or the storm planet. And of course, the dark planet just looked like a giant black smudge from the *Aurora*.

My thoughts are tinged with sadness. This is as close to the planet as I'm ever going to get. The captain will never allow me to participate in a landing party again. I won't have a chance to see those giant trees, or learn how the aliens communicate.

Sighing, I turn away from the viewport. It would be best to try and forget about the planet. The sight of the globe – knowing I will never have the opportunity to visit it – is too depressing.

"When do you go back on duty?" Wiggs asks.

"I'm sure Sharden will appear any second now," I reply drearily.

"Oh. It's been a while since we did any gaming," Wiggs says. "I was hoping…" his voice trails off.

"No," I say despondently. "I doubt I will ever have another chance to game with you."

The door swishes open. Wiggs looks up as Sharden enters. Apparently, he sees the smug gleam in Sharden's eyes, because he turns back to me and says, "No, I don't suppose you will."

―――――

Three days have passed with no change. We have maintained a high orbit, keeping well clear of the local space traffic. According to Kartak, the captain has insisted that we make contact with the aliens before sending down a lander. At this rate, our supplies will be depleted before we are able to successfully communicate with the aliens. And the scientists have run out of ideas.

I gaze out the viewport at the activity in orbit. Surely the aliens must communicate with each other in order navigate safely, and notify others of any change in schedule or plans. But how? I'm just as stumped as the scientists. Turning to Kartak and Wiggs, I say, "So what now?"

"We have to convince the captain to send the lander down," Kartak replies, rubbing his hand against the armrest of the couch he's sitting on. "We can't afford to delay any longer."

"What if they perceive the lander as a threat?" I ask, returning my gaze to the viewport. "It won't do us any good if the lander is damaged… or destroyed," I add reluctantly. If the lander gets destroyed, then whoever is inside it at the time will also perish. That would be just horrible.

"They've left the *Aurora* alone," Wiggs points out. "The lander is even smaller. There's a good chance they won't destroy it."

"Anyway, it's a risk we have to take," Kartak adds. "I'd be willing to pilot the lander."

"And I would go with you, if I'm allowed," I say. Despite the danger, I'm eager to see the planet. Plus, with Kartak at the controls, I'm confident we'd have a chance to avoid too much harm if things get ugly.

Kartak smiles. "I would certainly welcome that," he says. "You have proven skillful in communicating with alien species. That could be very useful down there."

I feel my chest swell with pride at the words. Looking at Wiggs, I say, "And what about you?"

"I sure wouldn't mind getting off the *Aurora* for a bit," he says. "I think now would be as good a time as any for another attempt."

"The captain should be done with the shields and environmental systems cross-check," Kartak says, standing up. "Perhaps we should offer him a little snack of strawberries. It might put him in a better mood."

"I can go get some," Wiggs says, pulling himself to his feet. "I'll meet you on the bridge in five minutes."

As they head for the door, I stretch out on the couch. Sharden shouldn't be coming for another ten minutes or so with my afternoon work schedule. That gives me a bit of time for a nap.

Just as I'm starting to doze off, the lounge hatch swishes open. I groan. It's time for another dreary afternoon of cleaning.

"Sean?" someone calls from the hatchway.

That isn't Sharden's voice. I pop up into a sitting position. Sure enough, Kartak and Wiggs are making their way toward my couch.

"The captain has finally caved," Wiggs says, grinning. "Kartak and I will be on the landing party."

"That's great!" I say, trying to muster up some excitement for them. They get to go explore, while I'm stuck here on the ship.

"We have to get ready," Kartak says. "We'll see you at the landing bay in one hour."

"Sure, I'll be there," I say.

"You'd better be," Kartak growls as he turns back toward the hatch. "Oh, and make sure your suit is charged and ready."

This puzzles me. Why does my suit have to be ready? "Sure," I say. I can hear the bewilderment in my voice. Evidently, Kartak does as well.

The crooked-fingered scientist pauses at the hatchway, and looks at me with a grin. "After all, we can't do without our communications specialist down there." With that he turns and disappears out the hatch, leaving me in stunned silence.

CHAPTER 6

Into the Tree

The view outside the lander viewport is astounding. I saw those two orbiting stations from the *Aurora*, but now that we're closer, I see just how cluttered the space around the planet is. Four large space stations are clearly visible against the backdrop of the globe. Dozens of smaller craft maneuver between the stations, or head off toward unknown destinations. What are the aliens like? Will they help us?

My thoughts turn to the sloth-bears and tulip people, two intelligent alien races I've met. They were both helpful. We can't expect all alien races to be like that. If a species turns out to be hostile, we shall have to recognize it quickly and figure out how to deal with them.

"How are your history lessons going?" Wiggs asks, shaking me from my thoughts. I turn to look at him. His eyes are crinkling with laughter.

"As dull as ever," I reply, trying to ignore his mirth. "The textbook is so boring."

Wiggs nods and strokes his goatee. "You need a proper teacher."

"Yeah, well I've had plenty of history teachers," I growl, thinking back to some of my classes in Victoria. "None of them have been much better than the textbook. Speaking of history, though, I was wondering if you could tell me more about Tanzania."

"Tanzania," Wiggs says, looking thoughtful. "A long time ago, Tanzania was a beautiful country: it had the Rift Valley, Mount Kilimanjaro, Lake Victoria, and abundant wildlife.

From what I've read, the people were kind and generous. But the country was extremely poor.

"A president named Mwamini changed that," Wiggs continues, shifting in his seat to face me better. "He helped the economy grow. He helped Tanzania become more industrialized, and broke the cycle of poverty. The most amazing thing, though, is that Mwamini was able to do this without destroying Tanzania's natural beauty. His policies actually helped preserve the natural wonders, and animal populations that had been in decline started to flourish. Many of the animals we have today may have become extinct if it wasn't for Mwamini."

This gives me a lot to think about. It's hard to know the truth about stuff that happened such a long time ago. A part of me wishes I could go back and see these events with my own eyes. Wanting to hear more, I say, "I wonder –"

"There's a pair of ships descending in front of us," Kartak says, cutting me off.

I crane my neck to look through the viewport. I spot two glints of light – the star reflecting off of metal hulls. The lead ship is already skimming the atmosphere.

"Do you plan to follow them?" Sharden asks.

"They will probably land near a town or city," Kartak replies. "That would be our best chance of finding supplies."

"What if they don't like being followed?" I ask, shifting uncomfortably in my seat at the thought of a confrontation.

"We'll keep our distance," Kartak assures me. "There's enough traffic that it shouldn't be a problem."

He sounds confident. I hope he's right.

We maneuver around a large station, keeping well clear of any flight zones they may have. The second ship enters the atmosphere. Despite Kartak's promise that we will keep our distance, we're not far behind.

As we enter the atmosphere, my stomach does a funny flip. It's kind of like what I feel when a ship folds, but slightly different. I also feel a lot heavier, as if gravity is three or four times as strong as it was a moment ago.

The first hint that something isn't normal, though, comes from my clothes. They grow suddenly tight. Seconds later, a great sound of ripping fabric echoes through the flight deck. Something has happened to my shirt, but I'm not bothered with that right now. I want to see every detail of this new world, so I keep my gaze focused out the viewport.

The lead ship is just a sparkle of light in the distance. It seems to be approaching a shadowy shape. The shadowy shape soon morphs into one, two, three, four huge trees. The second ship is still clearly visible ahead and to our right. I can't see the ground because of a thick layer of clouds.

As we get closer, I realize that *huge* isn't the right word to describe the trees. I'm not sure if there's a word in our vocabulary fit to describe their size. There is a flat surface in the upper canopy of the closest tree, ringed by thick green foliage twisting and waving in the wind currents. And on that flat surface are colorful objects... vehicles?

Sure enough, as I watch, the second ship glides down, hovers over the platform for a moment, and settles to the surface. A few seconds later, I see another ship lift slowly from the other end of the platform. After clearing the top of the tree, it banks left and speeds away. I follow the craft with my eyes until it disappears into a cloud bank. Turning back to the platform, I notice that something is happening: an empty section of the flat surface is glowing in expanding orange rings.

"I guess they're inviting us to land," Kartak mutters, and adjusts the lander's vector. Soon we are lined up with the landing pad.

As we hover momentarily over our spot, I try to count the vehicles – spacecraft, for the most part, some bigger, some smaller than our own – I can't see all of them, but there appears to be at least forty. Forty vehicles parked at the top of a tree!

After landing, I unbuckle my harness and try to stand. I can't lift myself up! The gravity must be really strong here.

Leaning to the right, I grab the seatback in front of me with my left hand, the armrest of my chair with my right hand, and haul myself to my feet.

Something is wrong.

Tearing my gaze from the viewport, I look down. My shirt is in tatters. My belly is spilling over the top of my shredded pants – it's huge! My fingers have turned into short sausages with nails half-drowned in flesh. My arms have swelled to about five times their normal size, with flab that jiggles with each tiny move I make.

I reach down quickly and grab my ripped pants, trying to cover up the best I can. As I try to figure out what to do with my clothes, my ankles, knees, and back start to ache under all of the added weight.

"What in the galaxy has happened to you?" Sharden asks, sounding astounded.

I'm about to reply, when I look up and realize his gaze is focused on someone else. I follow his line of sight, and almost drop my pants in shock.

Wiggs was sitting two chairs to my right during the lander ride. The person now sitting in that chair definitely isn't Wiggs. Yes, the wild red hair and goatee fit, but the rest of the body…

The person sitting in Wiggs's chair is skinny; the kind of skinny that some would call scrawny. He has sharp cheekbones, spindly fingers, and his body is absolutely lost in its clothing.

He quickly climbs out of his chair, turns around so that his back is to us, and lets his shorts drop to the floor. Then he puts both legs into one leg-hole of the shorts, pulls the shorts up, magically produces a pin from somewhere, and pins up the excess material. Now he is wearing a really weird skirt. Or I guess for him, it's a really weird kilt.

His shoulders aren't wide enough to keep his shirt up. Evidently, he is out of pins. Wiggs gives up on it after a couple of attempts and lets it slide down his body to the deck. Apparently, he will now be going around bare-chested.

"Tada!" he shouts, and turns around. It is so weird looking at a skinny Wiggs. He has gone from looking like one of the giant, house-sized balloons at a parade, to looking like the balloon animals you might see at a birthday party.

"It looks like Wiggs isn't the only one who's been transformed," Kartak comments, staring at me. "This is bizarre. I wonder if our metabolisms and fat storage have somehow been switched," he muses. Kartak's sharp mind is always working. "I know my clothes are feeling a little tight right now."

"Whatever is happening, it's a good thing it seems to operate within normal human levels for weight. Otherwise, Sean and I could have been dead ducks," Wiggs observes.

"Right, enough theorizing," Kartak says, leaping into motion. "We need to find Sean some clothes before he ends up like Adam on his first date with Eve."

Wiggs and Kartak search through the lander, but come up empty. That is, until Wiggs snaps his fingers and says, "I've got it! Sean can use my spacesuit. It might still be a bit big on him, but it will fit him a lot better than it would fit me right now."

I waddle into the cargo bay, overjoyed at the idea. Something to cover me up! I have to stop halfway across the bay to catch my breath. It feels like I'm climbing Mount Kilimanjaro.

It would be awful to be overweight and feel like this all the time. I'm glad I've stopped thinking bad things about Wiggs and his weight. I can't see how he manages. I have to make sure this never happens to me... assuming my body changes back once we leave this place. I had better get my proper body back!

After a few more steps, I'm standing in front of the suit locker. Kartak slides the door open, and Wiggs pulls the appropriate suit down. My joy evaporates when I catch a whiff of it.

The stench wafting out of Wiggs's suit is ten times worse than my own suit's. I can't remember ever smelling something so foul. I'm already having trouble breathing. What will it be like with that stench constantly around me? And I will have to endure it the entire time we're on the planet. Should I just stay in the lander? When the others leave, I could slip free of the suit. That would also mean a lot less walking with my heavy body.

But I want to stay with the others. I'm not sure how far the lander is able to transmit. I don't want to be out of contact with them. Plus, I want to see what these enormous trees are like. No, I shall just have to bear the awful stink.

I slip the suit on, grimacing at the thought of rashes and other health hazards I'm facing. The arms and legs of the suit are too long – I have to scrunch them up a bit – but it's actually not a bad fit. I'm so focused on the horrible sensations of the suit, I almost forget to grab my graphic pad. Turning back at the last second, I reach into the locker and find the suit I *was* going to use (I don't think of it as my suit – that is in the spare parts locker aboard the *Aurora* after getting shredded on the dark planet). I slip the graphic pad from the pocket where I left it in preparation for this mission, and slide it into a pocket of Wiggs's suit.

"Wiggs, here's one for you," Kartak says, tossing him a shiny new spacesuit. That's not fair! I have to endure his awful old suit, and he gets a brand new one.

"It's one of the lander's emergency suits," Wiggs says, seeing me eye the stiff clean fabric.

"Its systems aren't built for rugged use, and its oxygen supply is limited," Kartak says. "But it should work well enough for this place."

"According to the scanners the air here is breathable, right?" Wiggs asks, as he pulls the suit on.

"That's correct," Kartak says. "But let's make sure we don't have to put that to the test." After giving each of our suits a quick check, Kartak gives a satisfied grunt. "Right, let's head out."

I secure my helmet, sucking in my first lungful of truly putrid air. The breath catches in my lungs. I have to force myself to stay calm and breathe normally.

Kartak leads us into the airlock. The hatch seals behind us, the lock cycles, and Kartak hits the sensor for the outer hatch.

The door quickly slides open, revealing a row of tall green plants. They block my view of the vista around the tree. Pushing aside long fluttering leaves, I cross through the narrow band of plants. Beyond the vegetation is the edge of the landing platform. I stay well away from the lip, stand on my tiptoes, and peek over the side.

Below me, I see branches wide enough to comfortably fit full-size houses; I'm talking three bedroom, two baths, living room, family room, dining room – the whole works. Below those branches is a thick layer of clouds, swirling around the tree like a grasping white phantom. I shudder and sidle quickly away from the edge of the platform.

We weave between vehicles of all shapes, sizes, and colors. Most of them look well-used: dented, scratched, standing tilted on bent landing struts. There is one in particular next to our lander that looks like it is one or two hops away from the junkyard.

After several minutes, I catch sight of the tree trunk at the center of the platform. Even this close to the tree's summit, the bole is enormous. Half a dozen elevators could easily fit inside it.

There are ten or fifteen aliens of several different species gathered just outside the trunk, next to a collection of transparent spheres. As I watch, one of them touches a bubble. The transparent material quickly envelopes him. I stop in shock. He's been eaten, just like that!

The sphere rolls toward the trunk with the alien trapped inside. Curiously, the alien isn't struggling to get free. Could he be stunned?

The bubble touches the trunk at a spot that looks different from the rest of the surface: it is a translucent cream color, rather than the darker shade of brown of the surrounding trunk. The sphere pauses there for a moment, and then it seems to push its way into the tree. Several seconds later it disappears, leaving no evidence that it ever existed.

Another alien touches a different sphere. This alien, too, is quickly enveloped. His sphere rolls forward and enters the same place in the trunk.

Several yards around the trunk to the right, I spot a transparent sphere emerge from inside the tree. There is an alien inside this bubble. After a couple of seconds, the bubble seems to flow closely around the occupant. It looks like the sphere is smothering him. Still, the alien doesn't struggle. A moment later, the alien is standing *outside* of the transparent sphere. I stop and gawk as the alien lashes the sphere down, and then heads into the maze of vehicles on the platform.

"It looks like those spheres are some kind of transportation system," Kartak mutters. "I wonder how they work?"

"Each of the aliens is wearing something on one of their appendages," Wiggs says. "This is what they keep touching to the skin of the spheres before getting in or out. Maybe it is some kind of communication device."

"We need to get some if we're going to get anywhere," Kartak says, scanning the crowd.

"Can we trust those bubbles?" I ask. I don't like the idea of getting trapped in one.

"I don't think we have a choice," Kartak replies. "Every single alien is using them. If we want to get inside the tree, I think the bubbles are the only way in."

A sudden sound catches my attention. One of the aliens is staring at us and grunting. I take out the graphic pad and see if I can get a translation. Nothing appears on the screen.

"What do you think?" Sharden asks.

"He seems to be calling us over," I say, stowing the pad back in my suit.

"There are several more of his species over there," Kartak says, indicating a cluster of the aliens.

By this time, we are only a few yards away from the crowd. We stop in front of the alien. I focus my gaze on what looks like a cluster of eyes, and say, "What do you want?"

He grunts again.

"I'm sorry, we can't understand you," I say, shaking my head.

The alien grunts and holds up a long tentacle. He taps it with another tentacle. I notice that there's something wrapped around the first appendage. It looks like some kind of slug-like creature, with green skin mottled with black.

"That's what they use to enter the bubbles," Wiggs says. "Some kind of creature."

I jump as the alien wraps a tentacle around my wrist and sticks the slug-like creature in my face. "Hey, get that away from me! Let me go!"

The alien grabs Sharden's wrist with another tentacle. One of his companions slides over and does the same to Kartak and Wiggs.

"Relax, Sean," Kartak says. "It looks like they want to bring us inside."

Sure enough, the alien pulls me over to the clump of transparent spheres. Choosing a large one, he waves the slug-like creature in front of my face again. "Carg," he grunts, and then presses the creature against the wall of the sphere. Within seconds, the sphere flows around us and we are trapped inside. I'm glad for the protection of my spacesuit. I would not want this thing touching my skin, especially my face.

Our transparent bubble rolls toward the trunk. I have to scramble to keep from falling down. It's like walking on a curved treadmill.

We slide through some kind of membrane, and suddenly we're inside the tree. Faint light filters in through the membrane, but not enough to let me see my surroundings. We seem to be bobbing in some kind of liquid. We drift downward, and soon the last trace of light disappears.

We are left tumbling in complete darkness.

CHAPTER 7

Mist

Since I can't see, my hearing seems sharper: I'm surrounded by sloshing and creaking, as if I'm on a sailing boat. Disorientation sets in. I can't tell which way is up and which way is down. I try to turn on my headlamp, but the controls on this suit are unfamiliar.

A spark of panic is quickly building into a blaze. My thoughts race back to the dark planet, and all of the creatures that lurked out of sight. Are there beasts close by, waiting to pounce on me? I gaze wildly around, terrified that I will see the glint of light off of dozens of eyes. But what I see is far worse: the complete blackness continues. I have to get out of here! I can't stay in this darkness; it's too much!

I start clawing at the wall of the bubble, but quickly stop myself. We seem to be moving through some sort of liquid. If the bubble bursts, we'll get drenched. Would the liquid foul up my suit? I can't risk that. I must calm down!

The darkness stretches on. I can't see Sharden, or the alien, or even the hand I'm waving in front of my face. It's like I'm lost deep in the earth without a lamp.

The noises grow louder; it is completely overwhelming. I'm drowning in darkness and sound and revolting stench. My legs are trembling so much they won't hold me up much longer. I fall to my hands and knees. What I really want to do is curl up in a ball and shut the darkness out. But I force myself to remain on my hands and knees. I can't let the darkness master me completely.

The bubble starts to roll. The floor is quickly turning into a wall. Scurrying quickly down, I have to crawl with the movement in order to remain on the floor. An embarrassing picture flashes through my mind. I must look like a hamster in a ball. This isn't the kind of image I want people to associate with me.

The embarrassment is fleeting. The darkness drives all other thoughts and sensations away. It is absolute.

The dark planet again invades my thoughts: the complete, numbing disorientation; the feel of the rips in my back where the creature tore into me; the periods where my body couldn't decide whether it was freezing or burning.

A sudden glow cuts through the sphere, making my heart leap with joy. Finally, the darkness has passed! I rise unsteadily to my feet, hoping Sharden didn't notice me cowering on the floor. The bubble pushes through a membrane and rolls to a stop. The sphere flows down my body and I step out, gazing around in utter amazement.

We are in a broad corridor. The light is coming from several huge, segmented creatures that seem to be clinging to – or perhaps growing out from – the walls. The closest one is easily as large as a hopper. Each of the creatures emits light of a different color: deep amber, indigo, periwinkle, and one that's almost pearlescent. They are all soft and soothing.

Dozens of different species stride, slither, hop, or flow down the middle of the passage in what appears to be six distinct lanes of traffic, three in each direction. One has a large mouth that seems to take up its entire head, and a jelly-like body. It bounds along, hovering an unusually long time at the top of each bounce. Another creature catches my eye. I can't tell if its body is covered in fur, feathers, tentacles, or what it is. I also can't tell how it moves. I don't see any legs, but it doesn't roll or slither or bounce. A third species has four legs set in a circle on each side of its body. These spin around, almost like the paddle of an ancient steam ship, and propel it forward.

There are also many different types of insects, each with a distinct color pattern. But these insects are far bigger than anything we have on Earth. Most of them are as long or longer than one of my legs. Some of them are as big as me. The insects keep to the outer edges of the corridor, scurrying close to the wall.

As I look closer at the alien traffic, I realize that something is different about the two inner-most lanes. These beings aren't moving under their own power. Some are riding mounts (which differ widely in terms of size, shape, number of legs, and skin type). Others are being carried in sedan chairs or litters by teams of creatures. The inner lanes must be reserved for the most important beings.

Something bumps into me from behind. I turn and see that Kartak and Wiggs have joined us. The stupefied look on their faces is quite amusing, although my expression probably isn't much different.

The muted roar of clicks, hums, rumbles, and warbles is almost overwhelming. How do all of these creatures understand each other? This thought triggers something in my mind: the graphic pad! I take it out and scan the screen. The translation program is still running, picking up every vocalization around us, trying to make sense of it. Because a lot of communication is nonverbal, the program is also tied into miniature cameras on my suit. It can monitor the body language of beings around me. Has it heard enough of our alien guide's grunts and seen enough of its body language to communicate with it? I highly doubt it; the computer will likely need thousands of communication cues in order to build up context. But it's worth a try.

I type in the words *we need food and water* and hit enter. A few moments of waiting gives me the answer I've been expecting. The graphic pad is silent. It doesn't translate my sentence into the alien's grunting language.

I stow the graphic pad back in my pocket, just as the alien again grabs me with a tentacle and yanks me forward. My human companions receive similar treatment.

Using the outer lane of traffic – much too close to the huge insects for my comfort – we are led down the hallway, and then turn right into a new hallway. The glow-worms here aren't quite as big as the first ones I saw (they are about the size of small cars), but their colors are just as beautiful: emerald, magenta, reddish-gold, lavender. The walls are smooth, with no cracks or knobby outgrowths that I can see. Ovals of a different color from the surrounding wood are spaced evenly along the walls on both sides. A bit of observation reveals their function: I see an alien touch the middle of an oval. It dilates open, and the alien slithers through the opening. These must be doors to various rooms.

This corridor is much less congested, with only two lanes of traffic. My guide releases his grip on my arm. He must figure there isn't much chance of us getting separated here.

I slowly become aware of a faint screech rising above the background noise. It sounds like a rusted door that's being forced open, repeated over and over again. I turn down the volume on the external pickup in my helmet. The annoying sound disappears. Several strides later, the screech returns, growing louder every second. I hastily switch off the microphones, but the muffled sound still penetrates my helmet. It's a good thing I have the helmet on, otherwise the sound would be unbearable.

Suddenly, a multi-legged creature skids around a corner and sprints toward us, closely followed by the largest insects I've seen yet. After a few seconds of watching, I realize the mandibles of the two insects are twitching in time to the screeching. They must be creating the racket.

I jump heavily toward the wall with the rest of the crowd... just in time. The creature whisks past, almost ramming my hip.

As it draws even with me, one of the pursuing insects lunges forward and takes a swipe with its right foreleg; it connects soundly with several of the creature's rear legs. The beast stumbles and rolls awkwardly across the floor, nearly bowling over several other pedestrians.

I watch in fascination and horror as the insects rush to either side of the creature. Their screeching stops abruptly. The insects quickly turn their backs to the fallen alien and start to shoot webbing from their abdomens. After a moment, they somehow hoist the beast off the floor and start rolling him around and around – like a pig on a spit – coating him securely with the webbing. Now that it is completely encased, each insect grabs hold of the webbing with a forelimb, and they drag the captured creature out of sight.

My heart thumps loudly with shock and nerves. I glance at Sharden. He looks a little startled, but nothing like how I'm feeling.

As soon as the insects disappear, everyone around me starts moving along as if nothing happened. Such predatory attacks must occur often here. Is that what I just witnessed: a hunt, out here in plain view? Is this how the insects get their meals? If so, do they target certain species, or is everyone fair game?

Or was it something else... an arrest, perhaps? The thought is intriguing. Too bad I'll never know.

A tentacle wraps around my wrist and tugs at my arm. My guide – or one of his companions – appears to grunt something, but I can't hear it. I remember my pickups are muted, and turn the gain back up. I catch the alien's last couple of grunts, and then he sets off down the hallway. I have to trot to keep up.

We reach a cross-corridor. I start to step forward, but my guide restrains me with a thick tentacle. He grunts something unintelligible, waving his tentacles for emphasis. It's almost like he's chewing me out for not following his lead.

"OK, just relax," I say, even though I know he won't understand me. He grunts a few more phrases at me, slapping the side of my helmet with a thick tentacle. The alien's rant winds down. He turns to face the cross-corridor. Eventually, a gap opens up in the nearest lane of traffic. My guide pulls me forward and we join the flow of beings.

A couple of minutes later, the breath catches in my throat. The broad avenue we've been following opens up into an enormous room, like a concourse. The glow-worms in here are gigantic. Flowering plants and vine-coated trestles are dotted throughout the interior. I hear the sound of water – are there really fountains, here inside a tree? I don't see any, but that's what it sounds like. There are also streaks of colored light that pass overhead. It takes me a while to catch sight of their source. Eventually, one flashes by just a few yards ahead. It is some sort of flying creature. It passes too fast to make out more than a long, thin body like a glowing ribbon.

The colors here are so vibrant, they seem much crisper and brighter than anything on Earth. Has my time in the rainbow galaxy enhanced my ability to discern the richness and depth of the colors? Or does it have something to do with the kind of light the glow-worms emit?

I stand and watch the flashes of colored light crisscrossing through the great space. They dance between the trestles, zoom up and along the ceiling, skim low over the crowd... It is mesmerizing.

My alien guide tugs me forward. I take a step and stop, still eager to follow the ribbons of light. Evidently, this doesn't suit my guide. He yanks me forward so hard I almost sprawl on my stomach. After giving him a quick glare – which, of course, he doesn't understand – I fall into step with him. We enter a space filled with little wooden booths. It reminds me of an open-air marketplace. I crank my head around and reassure myself that Wiggs, Kartak, and Sharden are still with us.

Kartak catches my eye and says, "This might be our best bet for finding food. Keep an eye out, and see if you can determine their monetary system. I'm not sure what we can offer in exchange for food, but it would help to know what they use."

"How will we test the food to make sure it won't make us sick?" I ask, trying not to think about Kartak's experience with the tulip people's food.

"We'll just have to take what we can get and test it out later," Kartak replies.

We stop at a booth that is piled high with small purple orbs. I look closer, trying to figure out if they are some kind of fruit. My guide curls a tentacle around one of them and holds it out in front of me. What should I do? Is he expecting me to taste it?

Or is it something completely different, something that isn't even food? I turn to Kartak for advice.

"I'm not sure," he says, answering my unvoiced question. "See if your suit's sensors can get any reading on it."

I accept the purple orb and scan the unfamiliar screen of my suit. There is a sudden pressure on my shoulder. It's Wiggs. I take an involuntary step back. I still haven't gotten used to the sight of his gaunt face. Feeling foolish, I step forward to my original spot.

"Here, let me help you," he says, his face giving no hint of what he thinks about my reaction. The big guy types in a few commands. My screen fills up with information. I scan through it, note that the sphere is organic, and type in a query. The suit responds quickly.

"This is organic," I say. "And the suit suggests that there is a 96% chance that it is edible."

"That's a start," Kartak says, but he is interrupted by my guide, who starts grunting. The creature grabs my hand in a tentacle and shoves the fruit toward me. He starts grunting more forcefully. I quickly pull out the graphic pad with my free hand and check for a translation. Still nothing.

"What do you want me to do?" I ask, gazing into the alien's face. This is the first time I have really *looked* at the alien from this close: his eye clusters, his breathing slats, his moist, pulsing skin… My stomach churns at the sight, but I ignore it.

The alien continues to grunt and shove the fruit toward me. "Maybe it wants you to try it," Kartak suggests.

"Surely it realizes that I can't eat it through my visor," I say nervously. The alien is really getting insistent. What will it do if I can't fulfill its wishes?

"Perhaps they have helmets that allow certain things to pass through," Kartak says. "It might not know that you can't get the food through your faceplate."

Finally, the alien snatches the purple orb from my hand. It turns to Sharden and tries the same thing. After several minutes of this, it apparently gives up. Tossing the fruit back onto the pile, my guide grabs my hand and yanks me forward.

We stop at another stall. This one has brown, wrinkled, pea-sized objects that look like miniature walnuts. My guide scoops up several of the objects and shoves them toward me, grunting.

"Not again," I say with a sigh. I hold my hands down, trying to show that I can't accept it.

Another of the aliens starts grunting. A discussion – or perhaps an argument – breaks out between the two. The brown kernels are set back in their piles, and we are taken to another table. And then another. I'm getting as frustrated as my guide. We are supposed to be getting food. How are we going to communicate that to this alien if we keep refusing what it tries to give us?

Two of the aliens start grunting at each other again. A check of the graphic pad still reveals nothing. Are they going to abandon us here and get on with their own business? Will they try to find an interpreter? It's so frustrating, not being able to communicate!

"Have you picked up any sign of what they use for currency?" Kartak asks.

"Negative," Sharden replies.

"Not me," I say.

"I haven't either," says Wiggs.

"I wonder if they will allow us to take something and pay for it later," Kartak says.

"How would we ever communicate *that* to them?" Wiggs says dubiously.

"I don't know," Kartak admits. "We have to think of something."

I feel a sudden jerk on my arm. The aliens' discussion is over, and we are on the move again. We head away from the marketplace. I glance behind me at Kartak. He seems to be trying to stall his guide – and not having any luck at it. Are we heading for another marketplace, or did we miss our chance?

We enter a broad hallway lined with more booths. Our alien guides don't even hesitate. We pass quickly by and turn down a narrow side corridor, followed by a passage that is narrower still. This one is long, and barely wide enough for the two lanes of traffic.

At the far side, there is another collection of transparent spheres. I want to take a wide path around them – the memory of my trip through the darkness is still painfully fresh in my mind. Unfortunately, my guide doesn't cooperate. He heads straight for the cluster. Surely we don't need to make another of those trips!

Sure enough, my guide touches his slug-like creature to the skin of a bubble, and we are quickly enveloped. Panic is rising in my chest at the thought of the coming darkness. Isn't there any way we can avoid this? Do we have to continue on with these aliens?

The bubble rolls to a nearby membrane and passes slowly through. We are quickly wrapped in darkness. The bubble bumps against the side of the tube a couple of times. The sensation of pure terror is once again creeping over me, tightening its grip. I can't handle! – but a bright glow expands around the sphere, and we roll out into another hallway. All the tension drains from my body. This trip was much shorter than the last one.

We exit the bubble and continue on our way. Each twist and turn brings us deeper into the tree, farther from the safety of our lander. I hope my suit's navigational system has been able to chart our route, because I am completely lost.

We enter a dimly-lit hallway – I can only see three small glow-worms, and they are spaced a dozen yards apart. There are twisted, gnarled outgrowths on the walls, ceiling, and floor. Condensation trickles down the walls, and I spot numerous patches of an orange growth that looks like lichen. One of the glow-worms gives off a strange, pale tan glimmer. This area definitely has the feel of a rough neighborhood.

Halfway down the corridor, we stop in front of one of the ovals in the wall. It sags a bit in the middle, like spent elastic. My guide touches the center of the oval, and it slowly irises open.

I am led into a room a bit larger than the lounge on the *Aurora*. It is dark when we first enter, but then brightens almost immediately. The glow-worm in here is about the size of a rugby ball. A quick glance tells me that Kartak, Wiggs, and Sharden are close behind, as well as half a dozen of the aliens.

My guide picks up something from a cubic outgrowth of wood in the middle of the room; it appears to serve as a table. The object he holds looks like the cross between a shallow bowl and a genie lamp. He puts this up to his face and appears to take a drink. After giving a grunt, he shoves it toward me. My companions from the *Aurora* receive similar treatment.

"What do you think?" I ask Kartak quietly.

"We have to test one of these items sometime. It might as well be now. Plus, I get the impression we've offended them by refusing the things in the marketplace. If we don't accept this one, it might be pushing our luck too far," Kartak replies, his eyes fixed on one of the aliens. "Let me try it first. Wait and see what happens." Holding up his cup to us, he says "Cheers," and pours a bit into the liquid port on his suit.

"What!" I squawk in surprise, as my guide spins me around so that I can't see what's happening to Kartak. A tentacle holds me firmly around the middle. I try to twist away in horror, but the alien's grip is too strong. He jabs something into the liquid port of my suit. My muscles tense up, wondering what to expect. Nothing happens. My eyes track up toward the alien's face, to see if I can get a read on what it's thinking. I hear a hiss. A fine mist sprays my face. I take a reflexive breath in...

Instantly, the room starts whirling around, and then all goes black.

CHAPTER 8

The Vent

I open my eyes. Everything is dark. After a bit of fumbling, I find the activator for my suit's lamp and turn it on. My head feels like it's spinning. The smell doesn't help. It churns my stomach. It takes me a while to figure out that it's coming from my spacesuit. The room goes in and out of focus. I try to sit up, but this makes the spinning worse. I ease back down onto my back and try to take in my surroundings.

At first the disorientation is too overwhelming, and I can't see anything. After a few minutes, I'm slowly able to spot some features of my surroundings. I'm in a room with irregular walls; they curve inward and outward at random, like a three-dimensional puzzle piece. There are splotches of an orange substance that appears to be oozing from the walls. Condensation drips and trickles down the gleaming wooden surfaces.

A faint background hum slowly enters my awareness. I can't pinpoint its location or what's causing it. The sound seems to feed into my dizziness, making it worse.

I give up on exploring my surroundings. Lifting my left arm, I find the control for the lamp and memorize its location. Once I'm confident I will be able to find the activator when I need it, I switch off my lamp, and concentrate on trying to stop the world from tilting and whirling. The darkness is complete. There is no faint glimmer of moon or stars. The blackness seems to cut me off from everything I know. Right now, the only things that seem to exist are the thoughts inside my head.

A different sound reaches my ears, and a sudden light shines into the room, making me blink. I turn my eyes toward the source, and my blood freezes. It is one of the aliens.

I try to slide away from it on my back, but it's no use. It grabs my shoulder. I try to struggle, but my muscles won't obey me. The alien moves smoothly, almost casually, extracting a tube from its pouch. Then with a quick strike, it jabs something into my liquid port. Several seconds later, a mist hits my face, and darkness takes me again.

———

A moan escapes my lips. When I open my eyes, a complete blackness greets me once again. This can't go on. The blackness is too overwhelming. My fingers trembling, I switch on my lamp…

I'm in a completely different room. This one is tall and circular. The beam of my light doesn't even illuminate the ceiling. The chamber is also small – it's barely wide enough for me to lay fully stretched. Turning my head, I see that there is someone in here with me. The person is lying down, facing away from me. I can't see who it is.

I'm about to push myself up into a crouch when I jerk my right hand back; I almost put it straight down a hole in the middle of the floor. I shine my lamp across the opening. It is about ten inches wide. The light from my lamp doesn't reach the bottom. How deep does it go? What horrors are going to emerge from it at any moment? Surely it was made by one of those monstrous insects, or something even more horrible. I imagine a teeming pile of snakes slithering into our tiny chamber.

Taking a shuddering breath, I slide away from the hole and my back hits the wall. The opening sits there in the light of my lamp, like a brooding menace. Should I keep my lamp on? Would it be better to see if something is creeping from the hole, or to be oblivious to it?

In the end I decide to conserve the suit's battery. There's no telling how long it will be before I can recharge it again… if I'm ever able to recharge it.

My lamp snaps off. Now my only company is the sound of my breathing and the reek of the suit. I try to remember the brilliant colors of the tulip people, but it's hard in this caliginous world. Giving up on that, I decide to practice the sloth-bear's language. I tap something on my wrist, and then make a reply on my midriff and shoulder. I tap something else on my forearm, elbow, and hip, then make a reply on the side of my helmet (where my cheek would be) and my elbow.

I'm working through my seventh sequence of taps when it happens. I hear a slight sound, and a pink glow fills the chamber. Two of the aliens loom in the doorway. My back is already against the wall. There is no way for me to evade them.

Frantically, I turn so that my stomach is to the wall, and I cover up my liquid port with both hands. It doesn't do any good. Two strong tentacles roll me onto my back. Two more strong tentacles wrench my hands away from the port. Something is injected into my suit. A mist hits my face. And again, darkness greets me like an old friend.

———

There is a sharp pain in the center of my forehead. Is it split open? Do I have blood gushing out? I reach up to touch it, but my hand encounters something hard before it reaches my face. A helmet. I'm in a spacesuit. From the stench, I know it isn't mine. It hurts to think, but I try to recall what has happened... and where I'm at.

I am surrounded by blackness. Either I've gone blind, or someone has shut off all the lights. I try to gingerly sit up, but my head feels like it might explode. I immediately settle back down onto my back. I try to relax, so that my groggy mind can catch up to my current plight.

Wiggs. I'm using his suit. I can't quite remember why.

Fumbling around, I search for the activator for the suit's lamp with my fingers. It takes me several moments, but I finally manage to switch on the light. In its beam, I can see that I'm inside a cubic room, about three yards on a side. The walls are smooth, and appear to be made of wood. In front of me, there is an oval in the wall that is a slightly different color from its surroundings. Above and to the left of that is a set of slats that look like some kind of vent.

The room is bare apart from me and one other person. From this angle, I can't quite make out who it is. The figure doesn't move, and even the thought of speaking makes the pain in my head worse. I will save that puzzle for later.

I switch off my lamp, close my eyes, and let my mind drift.

When I wake up, my head is throbbing, but the pain isn't so bad. I also remember everything that has happened. And I wish I could forget.

Walls of wood suggest we must be in some room of the giant tree. Are we captives? We aren't bound in any way. Perhaps the effects of the mist were a mistake, something the aliens didn't expect due to our different physiologies, and we were left in here until the effects wear off.

But I seem to remember waking up two other times, in two other rooms. Did I dream that? I close my eyes and concentrate on the images. A room with irregular walls. A tall cylindrical room with a hole in the floor. The images are fuzzy, but they don't evaporate the way dreams do. I'm quite certain they are memories, not dreams. This was deliberate. Which means we are being held captive.

What will the aliens do? Will we be kept as slaves? Held as bargaining chips? Used as sacrifices? Eaten?

These last two thoughts make me sit bolt upright. Ignoring the ache in my head, I switch on the lamp and start to search through the pockets of my suit. My graphic pad is missing, as are the various knickknacks that Wiggs has stashed away over the years. The aliens must have cleaned it out. I check every pocket, just to make sure the aliens didn't miss one.

It turns out, they did.

There is a small pocket on the inside of my forearm. My gloved fingers are almost too thick to fit inside. There is something gleaming in the light of my lamp, though, and I'm determined to extract it.

It takes several minutes, twisting the suit, digging around, and twisting the suit some more, but at last a long, thin case clatters to the floor. I manage to grip it in my fingers, open it up, and peer inside.

It holds a multi-tool.

This could be useful. I snap the case shut and slip it into a pocket just above my left hip, where it will be easier to retrieve.

I check my oxygen level. The display shows just under three hours of air supply remaining. Everything else on the suit appears to be functioning normally.

Now it's time to see who my fellow prisoner is. I slide closer to the sleeping form and take a peek into the helmet.

It's Sharden.

Of all the rotten luck. Perhaps I should find a way to escape, and leave him behind. This thought is barely completed when his eyes snap open.

"It's about time you got out of bed," he snarls, pushing himself into a sitting position. "I've been waiting hours, but all you've been doing is snoring."

I take a breath and try to remain calm. "I can't help it that I've been asleep," I say. "Has anything happened?"

"There was a great holo-show, and then a huge feast, and then Wiggs, Kartak, and I decided to play Combat Zone," he says sarcastically.

"I'm serious. Has anyone come to check on us?" I ask, trying to hold back my temper.

"Oh, go cry to Mommy," Sharden replies. "Why did I have to get stuck with the tiny, snot-nosed boy?"

"Will you stop it!" I say sharply, resisting the urge to punch him. Why does he have to be so mean, especially now? "We need to work together! Your attitude isn't getting us anywhere."

"Well that's better," Sharden says with a smirk. "It looks like you're finally growing some spine."

This leaves me speechless. Is that what this has really been about since I got on board the *Aurora*? Sharden makes my life miserable because I don't show spine? That is absolutely ridiculous! I was the one who went down to the tulip people's planet and got the iridium, ran out of air, and had to brave the atmosphere. I got swept away from the lander on the ring planet, and had to learn to communicate with the sloth-bears. And I was the one who ventured out of the lander on the dark planet, surrounded by creatures I couldn't see, and got my back ripped open by their claws. How could anyone possibly say I don't have a spine after all that? Sharden must be insane.

But that's not important right now. I don't care what Sharden thinks of me. I just have to get him to cooperate somehow.

"Have you tried the membrane?" I ask, waving toward the oval in the wall.

"Yep," Sharden replies. "I tried touching it the way the aliens do. I've also tried pushing it, and banging on it, as well as various parts of the wall. It appears to be locked."

"How sturdy is the membrane? Do you think we could cut our way through?" I ask, peering more closely at the material.

"It's quite solid. Even if we had a blade, I doubt we could punch a hole in it," Sharden says. "Now a plasma torch might be a different story." Again there is sarcasm in his voice, but it seems more reflexive than intentional.

"Still, it's worth a try," I say.

"What, are you hiding a plasma torch somewhere in that suit? It's certainly gargantuan enough."

"No plasma torch," I reply, digging out the multi-tool case and opening it. "But this might come in handy."

"Where'd you get that?" Sharden asks, sounding impressed.

"It was in one of the pockets of the suit," I reply, flicking a blade open. "One our captors didn't see."

I test the blade out on the membrane. It barely makes a scratch. I try twisting the tip of the blade into the center of the membrane. It leaves a tiny mark.

"Looks like you were right," I say, closing down the blade.

I look around for other options. My eyes land on the slats. "I wonder what those are for." Stretching my hand up, I feel a slight pressure against the palm, as if there is air flowing into the room. "I think it's a vent of some kind."

"So, what about it?" Sharden asks.

"There is likely a tunnel for the air, kind of like a duct," I say, eyeing the slats. "If the tunnel is as large as the covering, one of us might be able to get through."

"It seems awfully small," Sharden says doubtfully. "On the other hand, we've got nothing better to do with our time."

I start sawing away at the lowest slat. The wood is hard. It takes several minutes to cut through one side of the slat. Switching hands, I start on the other side.

After finishing the first two slats, I hand the multi-tool over to Sharden. "You can reach the others easier than I can."

He takes the tool without comment (which for him is a big improvement) and gets to work. The task seems to go slowly, and I keep expecting one of our captors to come in and catch us in the act.

Finally, all of the slats are jumbled on the floor. There is indeed some kind of duct beyond the opening.

"Now what?" Sharden asks, peering at me as he returns the multi-tool to its case.

"With my current weight, I won't be able to fit in there," I say. "It's up to you."

"Yeah, I figured that out for myself," he says snidely. "There's just one little hitch in your plan."

"Your suit," I say, wondering if he'll balk at what I'm about to suggest.

"My suit," he replies. "It's too bulky."

"You'll have to take it off," I say.

He stands and stares at me for a long time without speaking. I can't tell what he's thinking, but I have a pretty good guess: I'm insane to think that he will take such a risk.

"You want me to take off my suit," he says at last, as if he doesn't believe it.

"Unless you can think of another way out of this mess," I reply. "Our air isn't going to last forever. We'll probably be forced to take our helmets off sooner or later."

Sharden stares at me appraisingly for another several minutes. Finally, he reaches up, unlatches his helmet, and lowers it gently to the floor. "You're right of course," he says, taking his first breath of the alien atmosphere. His nose twitches. Sharden takes a deeper breath, as if relishing the fresh air. He pulls his suit down and steps out of the boots. "Next problem. How am I supposed to get up there?" he asks, indicating the vent.

"I'll have to lift you up there," I reply, wincing a little on the inside. I'm not sure how I'm going to manage this. My legs are having enough trouble keeping my own bulky body up. If Sharden's weight is added to the equation, I'm not confident my muscles will be up to the task. Still, it must be done if we are to escape.

I get down on my hands and knees. "Climb onto my shoulders," I instruct him.

"I have a bad feeling about this," he says, as he steps across my body.

Bracing my hands against the wall, I get one foot under me and try to rise up. I manage a few inches, but that's all. I take several deep breaths. Then, gritting my teeth, I try again.

Slowly, wobbly, I inch my way up, and quickly get my second foot under me. Soon I'm standing almost straight up. Sharden thrashes around, knocking against my helmet several times with his thighs. It feels like I'm getting drilled into the floor. There is one more moment when he's driving my shoulders down – like an aluminum can getting crushed – and then his weight is gone.

"Got it!" he says, his voice muffled by the duct. "I sure hope this leads somewhere." Scrunching my back to ease the pain, I watch him scramble out of sight.

———

It has been over an hour since Sharden left. Surely he's had time to cut through the vent in the next room and get back by now. Perhaps the room is full of aliens. Even one alien would be a problem. With having to saw through the slats of a vent, Sharden wouldn't have any way to sneak up on it.

I sit back against the wall, running through various scenarios in my mind. Would Sharden be able to emerge if the aliens went to sleep? Thinking about the possibility that Sharden is trapped or has been recaptured, I rise back to my feet with nervous energy. I might have to find a way out on my own.

I poke and prod at the membrane, and then try tickling it in various areas. After that, I use a couple of different phrase combinations in the sloth-bears language. The membrane remains impenetrable. Of course, I hadn't really expected that to work.

Next, I run my gloved hands over the walls. It's extremely unlikely that there are hidden activators leading to secret passageways, the way there are in some of the more ridiculous holo-dramas, but I've got time on my hands and nothing better to do. My glove catches occasionally on small cracks or knobs, but most of the surface is as smooth as polished wood. There aren't any other vents, no holes in the floor or ceiling, nothing to get even the tiniest bit hopeful about. My examination brings me all the way back to the membrane. Not wanting to give up, I get down on my hands and knees, and explore the crease between the floor and wall. Again I come up empty. There aren't any tiny crevices, or any small doggy-door membranes for insects to pass through.

Worn out, I flop back down and huddle against the wall. A little more of my hope drains away with each passing minute.

Taking a sip of water, I try to come up with more options to try. But now that I don't even have the use of the multi-tool, I just can't think of anything.

Another thirty minutes trickle by. And another. I can't help the thought that bubbles up in my mind: Sharden has abandoned me. He has found a way out of the vent, but has decided it's too dangerous to come back. Or that I'm not worth coming back for. I am all alone.

Reaching the end of my air supply, I pop my helmet open and place it next to Sharden's. The alien air tickles my nose. I sneeze several times.

"Bless you," a voice says from my left, making me jump. I grab reflexively for one of the helmets. It's not much of a weapon, but it's the best I've got. An instant later, I realize a weapon isn't needed. The voice obviously wasn't coming from one of the aliens – I wouldn't be able to understand it if it was. Glancing over, I see Sharden peeking in through the membrane. I never even heard it open.

"You're finally back!" I say, rising to my feet and handing him his suit and helmet. He pulls on his suit as I grab my own helmet and step out through the opening. The light of my lamp reveals a larger room. There is only one other membrane. Could that be where Kartak and Wiggs are being kept?

As we walk toward the far membrane, Sharden explains, "The vent doesn't connect directly to this room. I had to exit in a different room and make my way back. I didn't have my suit to keep track of the distance I traveled in the duct. I also didn't know what the room outside our prison looks like, or how many rooms I would need to pass through to get to our little cell. It took several attempts to find our room again."

Sharden comes to a halt by the membrane and turns toward me. "Plus, the duct was dark and narrow," he says. "I couldn't use my lamp, otherwise the aliens would be able to see the light filtering through a vent. It was hard to move through the confined space, and I had to feel around for possible vents. I almost got stuck a couple of times. I definitely don't want to go on that joy ride again."

His description makes sense. It couldn't have been a pleasant journey. "Thanks for doing that, and thanks for coming back for me," I say, hoping he can hear that my gratitude is sincere.

"Yeah, well, we're not out of this yet," Sharden replies, touching the next membrane.

Instead of opening into another room as I expected, the membrane opens into a corridor. Dozens of insects scurry by. This brings me to a sharp halt. My stomach seems to sink to my feet. I figured Kartak and Wiggs would be kept in the same area as us. This doesn't appear to be the case. Where have they been taken? How can we possibly find them?

Gazing out into the corridor, I see that it is lit by giant glow-worms. I switch off my lamp to conserve energy. The scent of damp wood fills the air. There is a moderate amount of traffic in the middle of the corridor. The insect traffic is heavy along the edges. We wait for a break in the flow, and then step into the middle of the avenue.

"Any idea which way we should go?" I ask, a feeling of hopelessness trying to edge its way into my thoughts.

"I have no idea where the others are," Sharden replies.

I gaze in both directions, trying to find some inspiration. There are membranes lining the walls in both directions. Kartak and Wiggs could be in a room behind any one of them... Or they could be in a completely different part of the tree.

"It looks less busy this way," I say, pointing to the left. "We were moved from the room where they offered us the liquid, and a couple of other times as well. That might be easier to do if there are fewer people around." What I leave unsaid, is the fact that the insect attack on that multi-legged creature happened in the middle of a crowd. People here might not pay any attention to criminal activities. And other people in the corridor may not have even known a crime was being committed. They may have thought we were pets being taken for a walk.

"That doesn't really make sense to me," Sharden says. "But I guess we have to choose a direction, and that way's as good as any."

"Hold on a moment," I say, as excitement bubbles inside of me. It's weird that I haven't thought of this before. We've been in the rainbow universe so long, I've totally forgotten about radios.

I quickly settle my helmet into place, and activate my communication system. "Kartak? Wiggs? Can you hear me?"

There is a spit of static. That's it. Kartak and Wiggs don't have their radios on. Or they're unconscious. Or maybe something is blocking my transmission.

"Nobody home, huh?" Sharden says as I remove my helmet.

"Not now. I'll keep my radio on in case they try to make contact."

We set out side by side. I balance the helmet on my shoulder, keeping my ears pricked for any voice coming over the radio. After a few steps, I notice a sharp scent. It makes me think of campfires and barbecues. Smoke!

I look nervously around. A fire in the tree is the last thing we need right now. Where are the emergency exits? Does this tree even have any?

There aren't any flames or billows of smoke within my field of vision. None of the passing aliens is panicking or trying to get out of the hallway. There isn't any sign of a fire brigade rushing to the scene. They may have a special trick to keep fires contained in here.

After a few steps, the scent disappears. And there's still no sign of any flames. Perhaps the odor came from one of the beings that passed going in the opposite direction. Shrugging my shoulders, I forget about the smell, and keep my eyes open for any clue that might help us figure out where our friends are being held. I dodge around two beings coming from the other direction. They look like vaguely humanoid bags of jelly.

Focusing my eyes down the hallway, I feel my blood go cold. Two of the tentacled aliens are coming toward us! They seem to be deep in conversation. I'm quite certain they haven't spotted us, but that won't last.

"Sharden, over here, quick!" I say, grabbing his arm. Pushing through the scurrying insects, I touch the center of the nearest membrane. Thankfully, it dilates. A rotten stench hits my nostrils, but we don't have time to be picky. Sharden hurries through the opening, and I duck in after him. A few long seconds later, the membrane contracts.

My eyes quickly take in the interior. There are three small glow-worms on the walls. They flash on and off at random, like lightning bugs. To my right, there is a pile of what looks like pale violet gelatin in the corner. It pulses. With each pulse, something oozes out of it and trickles along the floor. In the opposite corner, there is another of these things. This one is quivering. Is it afraid? Excited? Angry?

The sight and smell are so revolting, I almost forget our danger. I start back toward the membrane, wanting to get out of here as quickly as possible. But then I recall why we rushed in here in the first place. We have to wait longer, to give the tentacled aliens plenty of time to pass this spot.

There is a sudden squeal from the pile of gelatin to my right, which makes my heart start to pound. Looking over, I see the thorax of an insect sticking out from the middle of the blob. I hadn't noticed this before. Is the jelly creature eating?

I glance over at Sharden. He looks pale and clammy, like he's about to be sick. "What do you think?" I ask.

"I think I'm never going to eat gelatin again," he says.

"No, I mean do you think we've waited long enough? Can we chance going out?"

"Let's give it another slow ten-count," Sharden replies.

I tick off the numbers in my head, trying to ignore the sights, sounds, and stench of the room's occupants. When I reach zero, I look quizzically at Sharden. He nods and opens the membrane. Standing a few feet back so that we are hidden in the shadows, we peek both ways down the hallway outside.

"I don't see anything," I whisper.

"I don't either," Sharden whispers back.

Moving slowly, we slide out of the room, keeping a wary eye out for possible enemies. "Looks clear," Sharden says. I nod, and we rejoin the flow of traffic.

Each time we come to a cross-corridor, I pause and look both ways, searching for anything familiar. It's hard to fight down the feeling of hopelessness rising inside me. The tree is just too huge. There are too many places to search. There's a feeling inside of me: that we are getting farther and farther away from where we were held captive; farther and farther away from Kartak and Wiggs. Should we turn around and search the other direction? Or perhaps down one of these cross-corridors?

I hold out my hand to stop Sharden, and put my helmet back on. "Kartak? Wiggs? Are you there?"

Again, the only answer is the spit of static. I close my eyes and count the seconds in my mind, willing something to happen, yearning to hear the voice of one of my friends. My count reaches 90. Sighing, I remove the helmet. Sharden doesn't even ask. He simply turns and trudges onward.

We come to the third cross-corridor. It is narrow and dim, with irregular walls… "Hey, doesn't this look like the hallway to that first room?" I ask, stepping out of the traffic lane and peering down the passageway. Are those orange splotches, or is it a glow-worm? I can't quite tell.

"Could be," Sharden grunts. "Or it could be one of hundreds of passages that I'm sure are just like it."

"I think it's at least worth a try," I say, trying not to let his skepticism get me down. Kartak and Wiggs have probably been moved from that original room like we were, but it would at least give us a place to start. *If* this is the right corridor, and *if* we can find the right room.

Sharden shrugs. "Sure, why not. We don't have anything better to do."

We slip into the narrow corridor, with Sharden off my left shoulder. I walk slowly, gazing at the walls, trying to spot anything familiar. Up ahead there is an orangish-tan glow-worm, kind of like a peach. I seem to remember seeing one like it before. This gets my hopes up a bit.

We are passing by the eighth or ninth membrane when I catch a whiff of something. I know that smell! "Stop for a moment," I tell Sharden, and sniff around to see if I can find where the smell is strongest. The reek from the suit makes this difficult, but after a moment, I'm able to narrow down the possibilities to three membranes. They all sag a little. Sharden nods with understanding.

"Wiggs has come this way. And recently," he says.

"He must have been transferred to a different room. Which membrane do you think he went through?" I ask, examining our three options.

"The middle one," Sharden replies, reaching for it, causing the flow of insects to divert around him.

"Do you have the multi-tool ready?" I ask. It's not much of a weapon, but it's the best we've got.

"Good idea," he says. Before opening the membrane, he reaches into a pocket and pulls out the tool. "Ready?" he asks.

"Yes," I say, though not very truthfully. My legs are shaking and my arms feel weak. How many of the aliens are we going to face inside?

The membrane dilates. The interior is dimly-lit by a single glow-worm. This appears to be the room where we were given the drink. It is empty. There is a membrane in each of the walls. A quick investigation reveals that the garlic smell gets stronger as I head toward the membrane in the right-hand wall.

Sharden stops, his hand poised to touch the membrane. He raises his right eyebrow. I nod. My muscles tense in anticipation. He touches the membrane, and it irises open.

Wiggs and Kartak are kneeling on the floor with their heads bowed forward. Three of the aliens are looming over them. My heart starts hammering in my chest. Just what I've been dreading: we are going to have to fight our way out of this.

CHAPTER 9

The Crossing

Sharden is on the first one in a flash. I head for the second alien, not sure what I'm going to do. Kartak launches himself at the third one.

I get a grip around the lower appendages of my alien and try to tackle him. It doesn't work. Thick tentacles wrap around my waist and start to squeeze. I flail around, trying to loosen its grip. I see Wiggs lash out and hook his fingers into a set of the alien's breathing slats. My opponent grunts and drops me. Two of his thickest tentacles whip around and send Wiggs flying onto his back.

The alien pounces forward, tentacles writhing, ready to grab or pummel the big guy. I catch my breath and dive back in, searching for some way to help Wiggs. Based on the reaction to Wiggs's attack, I'm quite certain the breathing slats are sensitive. Keeping my hand open and fingers flat, I jab at them from behind, trying to drive my fingers into the gaps between skin flaps as Wiggs had done. My strikes land off target, but they distract the alien enough for Wiggs to regroup.

The tussle lasts for several minutes. In the end, there are three aliens lying unconscious on the floor. Sheer desperation is probably what has given us the necessary strength to win.

"It's great to see you guys," Wiggs says, beaming. "I have no idea how you found us."

"Bedtime stories can wait until later," Sharden says sharply. "We have no idea how long these uglies are going to be out."

"He's right. Let's get going," Kartak says.

The crooked-fingered scientist takes the lead. When we get back to the corridor, he turns left. I'm not sure if he is going to try to retrace his steps to the lander, or if he's just trying to get us as far away from the alien's room as possible. As I walk I scan the area ahead, tense for any sign of danger.

Something is approaching. I can't figure out what it is. It looks almost like smoke, but it's moving in one of the lanes. The closer it gets, the more certain I am that it's some sort of alien. I can't tell how many there are – at times it looks like three or four distinct shapes, at other times it looks like one thick column of smoke. The outline of the creature isn't well defined, and seems to change constantly.

A sudden jabbering makes me look around in alarm. My muscles relax when I realize it's only an alien urging on its mount. Just as I'm about to turn my gaze back up the corridor, I ram into something that knocks me off my feet. I hit the floor with a thud that hurts my backside. What did I run into? After gazing around for a moment, I realize the only thing near me is the smoke-being. That's what I must have collided with. How can something that looks so much like smoke be so solid? It's weird.

"Are you okay, Sean?" Kartak asks, coming back to where I'm sitting.

"I think so," I say.

His eyes do a quick scan of the corridor around us. "Good. We need to keep moving," he says, stretching out his hand toward me. I grasp it, and the crooked-fingered scientist helps me back to my feet. Wiggs and Sharden are waiting a short ways up the corridor. They both look tense and anxious. Like me, they must be expecting to come across one of our captors at any minute.

We turn to the right and enter a kind of rotunda. There is a tang wafting across the room, like fresh-cut mango. The middle of the rotunda is filled with what appears to be pens full of fussing creatures. If this was Earth, I would have guessed it is some kind of cattle auction. There's no telling what the aliens do here, though.

As we get closer, an odor like wet-dog hits my nose, making it wrinkle. I don't have time to inspect the pens too closely, though. Kartak is already striding quickly down the concourse to the right. His instinct seems to urge him across the wide space as quickly as possible. This suits me just fine. We are too exposed here. I push my chubby legs as fast as they will go, trying to keep up. As I hustle in Kartak's wake, my eyes scan the rotunda, alert for any place an enemy could be lurking.

We skirt the penned-up animals (I'm quite sure none of our captors are concealed in there), pass by a group of small beings climbing various structures – an alien playground, perhaps? – and are now more than halfway across the concourse.

"Looks like trouble to the right," Kartak warns. I look over. A pair of unfamiliar aliens is standing by a domed structure next to a hallway entrance. They aren't pointing at us like a human might, but they are staring in our direction. Somehow I get the feeling they are excited – and not just because this is their first time seeing humans. It's almost as if they are expecting some action. Perhaps it's just my nerves feeding my imagination. I certainly hope so. The two aliens don't move toward us, but I keep an eye on them as I chug along.

A few seconds later, something emerges from the corridor behind them, and my blood freezes. "Come on!" Kartak shouts, and we break into a run. I stare at the newcomer – one of our enemies, bustling as if he's been summoned.

I glance ahead to make sure I'm still with the group. The other three have a bit of a lead. Willing my legs to pump faster, I try to put on a spurt of speed. Straight ahead there is a long, wide corridor. This is a major thoroughfare, with beings of all shapes and sizes filling the traffic lanes. I focus on getting there, trying to block out the thought of the alien to my right.

A dozen more steps and I'm in the corridor. Following Kartak's lead, I join the outermost lane. We slow down a bit due to the congestion. I wheeze to catch my breath, not daring to look back, afraid that at any second, I might feel a tentacle wrap tightly around my neck.

This corridor is giving me the creeps. I'm not sure which is worse: in the rotunda, we stuck out like a giraffe in a pizza parlor. In here, even though the passage is wide, I feel hemmed in. It would be easy to ambush us.

"Keep an eye out for those transparent bubbles," Kartak says over his shoulder, breaking into my thoughts. "We need to get off this level as soon as possible."

I scan the corridor ahead. There aren't any intersecting passages in my field of vision, much less a place that might have the transparent bubbles. There is something else up there, though. Two gargantuan creatures are approaching. They take up almost four lanes of traffic. Their skin shimmers, and seems to change color as they move. As the creatures approach, I notice that the nearby insects seem skittish. I don't blame them. There isn't much room between the huge creatures and the wall. The insects have to time things just right or risk getting squashed underfoot.

The creatures are almost even with us now. Are they mounts? It's hard to tell from my angle. As they lumber by, I try to catch a glimpse at their backs. I don't see anything up there.

Then a thought crosses my mind: do these creatures fit in the transparent bubbles? What if one of them gets stuck, clogging the tube? Would all of the creatures trapped behind them in the tube die in the utter darkness? The thought sends a shiver up my spine. I can't imagine that the tubes between the levels of the tree are big enough for these creatures. Perhaps there is another way into the tree, like a cargo entrance.

The behemoths are past. There is a clear view of the corridor ahead. And a clear view of something that paralyzes me. There are two beings from the species that imprisoned us! They are at the far end of the corridor. We have enemies in front and behind us, and most of the nearby aliens are shorter than we are. There is no way to get lost in the traffic.

As I'm thinking through our options, one of the aliens turns his head. He's spotted us! I see him speak briefly to his partner, then grab something from a pocket of his robe. I look left and right, desperate to find an escape route. There! To the right there is a membrane. Does it have another exit, or will we be trapped in a room? There's no time to worry about it. We have no choice but to risk it. Kartak has spotted the membrane as well. He is already reaching out to open the portal.

I dodge toward the membrane. There is a flash of light and a loud crack. The alien has fired a weapon. The discharge goes wide, hitting the wall with a mini explosion of electrical energy that definitely does not look healthy.

We pile through the membrane. I hear the crack of another near-miss behind us and duck down reflexively. Realizing I'm no longer in the line of fire, I straighten up and take a look around.

The room we're in is large. The floor is soft and weird, like I'm on a carpet of thick velvet. There is a lot of movement up ahead. It takes my mind a moment to figure out what's happening: a large group of leafy-scaled aliens is scattering to the walls, hissing and rustling.

"Let's go!" Kartak shouts, and starts running through the vacated space. The rest of us charge after him. There is a membrane on the far side of the room, slightly off-centered to our left. We come to a pounding halt and Kartak touches the center of the membrane. It opens to reveal another corridor. We pause just inside the room, taking in the lay of the land.

"I don't see any other membranes," Kartak says, his eyes scanning both ways down the hall. "There does seem to be a cross-corridor up on the left, but that may lead us straight into the aliens' tentacles."

"We can't stay in here," Sharden says. "They might come up from behind. Or these walking leaf piles might realize they outnumber us and become aggressive."

"Let's head to the right and hope it doesn't lead straight back to the rotunda," Kartak says after a moment. "Sean, keep an eye out behind us."

I walk sideways so that I can watch our backs. I've only gone a few steps when an enemy rounds the corner, followed by three more. It appears they were able to call in reinforcements.

"We've got company!" I say, as my heart begins to pound. One of the aliens raises a weapon. "He's going to fire!"

I duck down, presenting the smallest profile possible. The loud crack of the weapon never comes. I look back. The aliens are rushing toward us. I let out a startled yelp as a giant insect flies out of nowhere and tackles the leader, but the others don't even break stride.

"Come on, Sean, let's move!" Kartak shouts. "We have to find a way out of here!"

Keeping my head down, I sprint after him. A shot explodes to my left, and another hits the ceiling above me. I scan both walls, desperate to find a way out of the hallway. There are no membranes, and no cross-corridors.

Dodging through traffic, I know it's only a matter of time before the aliens catch up to us. Or before they manage to hit us with one of their weapons. What will they do? Put us back in a cell, or skip straight to carving us up for dinner?

I almost pass right by before I see it: to the left, there's a crack in the corridor wall. Will it be big enough for us to fit through?

"This way!" I shout, and dive for the narrow opening, just as more bursts of energy erupt around me. A couple of aliens in the next lane tumble down, thrashing in pain. My heart wrenches at the sight. I want to help them, but there's nothing I can do.

The opening is bigger than I thought. I waddle in sideways, wishing I was my typically skinny self. I manage to squeeze through without much difficulty. After about a yard, it widens enough for me to walk normally.

"I'd hate to see what one of those things does to human tissue," Sharden says, squeezing into the crack after me.

"Did we all make it?" I ask over my shoulder, as I shuffle farther in.

"We're all here," Kartak calls. "No one was injured."

I breathe out a sigh of relief at this news. Even so, we aren't safe yet. I have no idea where this crack leads... if it leads anywhere at all. We might hit a dead end, and get trapped from behind by the alien monsters. The thought sends a shudder through my body. How fast can the aliens move through narrow places? How long will it be before they are close enough to fire their weapons?

A faint rustling reaches my ears from up ahead. I can't identify what it is. And it doesn't matter, anyway. There is no choice but to keep going. After several more yards, there is a sharp curve. Sucking in a deep breath, making myself as skinny as possible, I squeeze around the bend, stumble into a wider passageway... and discover the source of the noise.

I am standing in the middle of an alley teeming with insects. Their chittering raises goosebumps on my arms and neck. I also hear a constant rasp that I eventually identify as hundreds of exoskeletons rubbing against each other. The insects flow around me, often brushing up against my legs. I want to get away from them! But the only way to do that would be to go back and face the aliens...

My fear of the aliens overpowers my revulsion of the bugs. We have to get as far from the entrance as we can before they arrive. Forcing my legs to move, I stumble forward, wading through the mass of oversized insects.

"What the devil?" I hear from behind. Evidently, Sharden likes sharing the path with insects as much as I do. "Great. We escape firearms, only to face death-by-overgrown-bugs," he growls.

"They don't seem to be bothering us," I point out, although this hardly makes me feel any better.

"Just wait until we get closer to their nest," Sharden snarls.

I hadn't thought of that. This area must be where the insects live. Will they attack us if we get too deep into their territory?

"Let's just keep moving and find another way out," Wiggs says.

The light is dim – the glow-worms I spot are all the size of my arm or smaller – but I can make out holes in the wall every fifty yards or so. I gaze into each one as I pass. They either go up or down. None of them head toward the interior of the tree.

The mass of insects seems to somehow grow even denser. I want to scream. How much longer can I stand this?

"It looks like there's only the one entrance on this level," Sharden says.

"That would be a poor design, if it's true," Kartak replies.

"Who says this tree city was designed?" Sharden snaps back.

"The evidence we've seen so far indicates –"

"I see something!" I shout. "There's a brighter light up ahead."

"That doesn't mean anything," Sharden replies sharply.

"It might," Wiggs says.

We hurry forward. As we get closer, I see that the light is coming from a gap in the ceiling. Several insects are crawling out. It takes my eyes a moment to adjust to the relative brightness, but then I see a sliver of blue speckled with green. The sky! Leaves!

"That hole leads outside!" I exclaim. I've been in this tree for so long, my body is craving fresh air and wide-open spaces. Just a glimpse of the outside world gets me quivering with anticipation.

"Let's climb up and see what we have," Kartak says.

I go first. Kartak and Wiggs each grab a side under my arm, and hoist me up. The opening is narrow, but I manage to squeeze through.

I immediately wish I was back with the insects.

I'm on a great branch. I catch glimpses of the ground through breaks in the clouds. I'm at least several hundred yards up, and there aren't any guardrails or other safety features. One slip, and I plunge to my death. Occasional gusts of wind seem eager to help me meet this fate.

"Move it, will you!" Sharden demands, his head poking through the slot.

I put my right hand inside my helmet and carefully crawl forward several yards, pushing my helmet forward as I go, my arms and legs feeling like soft rubber. I want to close my eyes, but then I might take a false step.

The branch stretches before me. In fact, it seems to extend all the way to the next tree. Is this actually just one tree with two trunks? Or have the branches somehow grown together? I notice that the branch narrows toward the middle, appears to be the same diameter for about ten yards, and then thickens as it gets closer to the other trunk. Somehow, the people who carved out the trees must have connected the branches as well, so that they could pass from one tree to another without going all the way down to the ground.

Soon the other three have clambered out and are perched on the branch with me. "Quite a view," Kartak comments. And then, after a moment's pause, he says, "I wonder if we can see the lander from here."

I gaze toward the treetop. No matter how I turn my head, there are too many branches blocking my line of sight.

"It's no good," Kartak concludes, obviously stymied by the foliage as well.

"Perhaps if we use one of those ramps, we might find an exit onto a higher branch," I suggest.

"Those holes looked awfully tight," Sharden says. "I'm not sure we would fit."

"It's the best option we have," Kartak says. "We have to give it a try."

The others start toward the entrance. I take another look at the tree on the far side of this branch. Off in the distance to my left, it looks like there is a branch that connects that tree to another one. There must be an entire network of trees.

I'm about to turn around and follow the others, when I catch a glimpse of something. I do a double take, and peer at it for a moment. My heart sinks.

"Uh, guys, I'm not sure – and I hope I'm wrong – but isn't that the landing platform over there?"

"What?" Kartak says, pausing in his descent – his legs are already in the entrance slot.

"That next tree over," I say, pointing to the crown of the neighboring behemoth. "I think that's the landing platform. Or another one just like it."

Kartak slides back out and puts his helmet on. For a moment I wonder what he's doing. Then I realize he must be using the zoom function in the helmet's visor.

"Sean's right," he says after a moment. "I can see the lander over there to the right."

"One of those skinny hallways they led us through must have been this branch," Wiggs says thoughtfully. "We have to search for it. But I don't like the thought of returning to the main part of the tree. Not with our alien friends looking for us."

"I think it would be better if we crossed up here," Kartak says. "The branch is plenty wide."

I gaze along the length of the branch, and my whole body turns to jelly. "Please tell me you're joking," I say, trying to decide which would be worse – to go inside and risk encountering the aliens, or to cross the branch out here with no safety net. I can't believe this is happening to me. If only I had the climbing claws I used on the tulip people's planet, that would at least make me feel a little better.

"What if there isn't an entrance into the tree on that side?" Sharden asks.

"I'm pretty sure the insects have exits along most of the branches," Kartak replies. "Especially important ones like this."

"Even so, it would be a nasty shock to go all that way and find we can't get in," Sharden growls.

"It's a risk we have to take," Kartak says firmly.

It's bad enough that we have to use this branch to cross to the next tree. But what if Sharden's right? What if we get there and find that there's no way in? I don't think I would have the nerve to cross back over to this tree. Perhaps it would be better to go back in right now and brave meeting the aliens.

Unfortunately, it's too late for this. Kartak is already striding along the branch as if he's walking across a wide plain. Wiggs and Sharden set out a little more cautiously. Rising shakily to my feet, I take several deep breaths, try to convince my muscles to work normally, and start to shuffle behind them.

The branch narrows. Soon I get back down onto all fours and start crawling like a baby. A gust of wind hits my right side. I try to get as low to the tree as possible. My muscles tense, waiting for that fatal moment when I get shoved over the edge. After a second or two, the wind dies down again. This doesn't make me feel any safer. By the time I reach the middle, I'm practically slithering on my belly.

Another gust of wind hits me. I have to stop and take a few breaths. I fight the urge to look down. I know if my eyes see the drop, it will paralyze my muscles and make it almost impossible to move. Kartak has already reached the other tree. Wiggs and Sharden aren't far behind. I still have fifty yards to go.

The wind is picking up, whipping all around me. The branch is groaning beneath me. I'm not going to make it. I'm going to fall. I just know it.

Again I pause. After taking a few breaths, I try to get going again. My muscles won't respond. I'm frozen in place. The wind is really lashing against me now, pushing me toward the edge.

"I'm with you, Sean," a voice says. "You can do it." I look up. Kartak is standing a few feet away. He has come all the way back here for me. "Come with me," he says.

He takes two steps and stops. I crawl forward a bit. He takes another two steps. I crawl a bit more. Kartak stays near me, encouraging me through each little stretch.

At long last, I've made it. The enormous trunk of the tree is just a few yards away. Wiggs shifts his feet a bit as I approach, bringing something into view. A flood of relief washes through my body at the sight. Just beyond Wiggs, there's an entrance! I can't wait to get back inside.

Yet even as this thought crosses my mind, a flurry of movement reminds me of what's to come: several insects emerge from the slot and head toward the trunk. Great. In my fear of falling off the branch, I forgot that going back inside means going back to the teeming insects. My relief evaporates at the thought.

CHAPTER 10

Pursuit

I wait for the others to slip through the hole. Taking a deep breath, I slowly crawl into position, tensing at each gust of wind. Once I reach the slot, I ease down to my belly – I don't have far to go these days – and slowly back blindly into the opening. I feel a moment of panic as my feet flail around, not touching anything.

"Hold still, will you!" Kartak demands.

I stop kicking my feet. A hand grabs my ankle. At the same moment, I start to slip. I almost drop my helmet in my panic. Clawing at the branch with my left hand, flinging my helmet around with my right, I try to stop myself. But the surface of the branch is smooth. There's nothing to grab. My back scrapes against the top of the opening, I plunge for an instant, and then my feet slam into the floor of the tunnel. I tumble to my back. Pain stabs through my ankles, shins, and knees. I huff and puff, trying to catch my breath.

Kartak hovers over me, the right side of his face lit by the exit, the left side of his face in shadow. "Are you okay Sean?" he asks.

"I don't know," I manage to pant out. "Give me a moment."

A couple of insects use me as a bridge. Several hard feet poke my face as they pass. I start to freak out again. This is all the motivation I need to will the pain away. "Okay, I'm ready to move… if I can get up, that is."

Kartak and Wiggs each grab an arm and help me lumber to my feet. My knees and ankles still ache, but it's bearable.

A. A. Akibibi

Before long, we reach the nearest ramp angling upward. It is indeed a tight fit, but we manage. Kartak leads, followed by Sharden and Wiggs. I take up the rear.

At first I wonder if the smooth surface might be too steep. But though the angle is challenging, the climb is possible for someone who is determined. And I am determined.

The smell and the darkness of the tunnel are horrible. Worse still, though, are the dozens of insects that keep scurrying up and forcing their way past me, despite the tight quarters. The sharp jabs of their feet on my arms, legs, and body remind me of my last game of Stratagem back on Earth: when Hoss was hitting me with everything he had. That was a game, though. This is a nightmare.

The tunnel seems to climb forever. My arms and legs start feeling dull, and my knees experience a new kind of ache from all of the crawling. What if this tunnel doesn't lead to another level? What if it simply ends in a pocket of the tree the insects use as a bedroom? Thoughts of a small cave packed with crawling, chittering insects gives me goosebumps. Will this insanity ever end?

Just as this thought crosses my mind, I see Wiggs twist to the left. A moment later, I realize I *see* Wiggs twist to the left – meaning there is light coming from somewhere.

Another yard and I see it: an exit on the left side of the tunnel. I force my bulk through and plop to the floor, exhausted. "I need to rest," I say, rubbing my legs and groaning.

"Let's take a five-minute breather, no more," Kartak says.

It seems like much less than five minutes before I'm using Kartak's arm and a wall of the tunnel as braces, as I heave myself to my feet. I plod at the rear of the group; it feels like I've climbed ten Kilimanjaro's during our escape.

"There's another ceiling exit," Kartak says, coming to a halt. An occasional insect crawls in through a slot in the ceiling. The leaves they carry flutter as they enter, and then hang limply as they reach the floor. There must be a breeze snaking in through the opening.

"I… I suggest… only one… of us goes… this time," I say, wheezing to catch my breath.

"I concur," Sharden says immediately. "I vote on Sean."

"I second that," says Wiggs.

"Looks like it's official," Kartak comments dryly.

This is definitely not what I had in mind. Kartak is the logical choice. But I can't tell whether they are joking or serious, and I'm not going to give them the satisfaction of seeing how much I dread going out.

"Fine," I grumble. "But you will have to hoist me up."

"I'll go," Wiggs says, chuckling and waving me back. "I'll see you in a bit."

Sharden and Kartak boost him up through the exit. A few seconds later, his head reappears.

"I can see the landing platform, all right," he says, grinning widely. "And the lander is almost directly above us. The branches that support the platform are about three layers up from here."

"Great," Kartak says. "Let's take another ramp. We'll see if we can find an exit to a branch near the platform."

Wiggs wiggles down, and bounces on his feet as he lands. "It feels great to be light!"

I know what he means. I would give anything to have my regular body back. My suit is sagging, my ankles are killing me, and I'm still trying to catch my breath from our climb.

The others start out down the corridor, searching for a tunnel leading upward. Not wanting to get separated from them, I take another two deep breaths, then forge ahead, wading through a river of scurrying, oversized insects. I start out slowly, so I can dodge the frantic critters all around me. After a few minutes, though, the others are getting farther ahead, and the corridor is getting even more packed. Pretty soon I might lose sight of Kartak, Wiggs, and Sharden. I don't want that to happen!

Picking up my pace, I shove insects out of the way, wincing at the sight of all the sharp mandibles around me. What if they get angry and decide to attack? They could probably chew through my suit within minutes. By the time the others realize I'm in trouble, I would be lying on the floor, with huge insects swarming all over me.

Panicked, I start to jog, bulling my way through the jammed tunnel. When I finally catch up to the group, I can hardly catch my breath. They have found another ramp leading upward. Kartak is already crawling through the narrow opening. I double over, panting as I wait for each of them to squirm into the tunnel.

My breath comes in great wheezing gasps. I can't seem to get enough air into my lungs. But I don't want to be left behind. Lurching forward, I hunch down, and crawl onto the ramp. Several insects try to squeeze past me, and get half-squashed against the tunnel mouth. I will never get used to being in such a tight space, with dozens of huge bugs crawling around me.

This ascent seems much longer than the last one. I don't feel like I have any strength left. It takes all of my willpower to just keep slowly moving one hand, and then the other. If this ramp climbs much farther, I'll be high enough to enter orbit around the planet. Will I see the *Aurora* gliding past as I crawl out of the tunnel?

Finally, I see Sharden turn left in front of me. With my last ounce of strength, I heave my body through the tunnel exit, and collapse to the floor.

"Right, let's find a –"

"Sean needs a bit of a breather," Sharden cuts in on Kartak.

Kartak glances at Sharden. There is a hint of surprise on his face, which he quickly hides. Kartak is undoubtedly as shocked as I am that Sharden would show concern for me. The crooked-fingered scientist turns toward me, holds my gaze for a moment, and then nods. "I'll scout ahead for an exit. The rest of you wait here."

Without waiting for a reply, he turns and plows through the flow of insects. I pull my left arm out of its sleeve and start scratching. The suit is starting to chafe – actually, it's been chafing for a while, but now it has reached the point of getting really annoying. I can't wait to get back to the ship and pull it off.

When Kartak returns, he looks pleased. "The exit's just around that bend," he says, pointing in the direction he came from. "I was able to pull my chin up through the opening and have a peek out. We are on one of the branches that support the landing pad. It looks like just a bit of a climb to get onto the platform itself. Plus, there is a row of vegetation at the edge of the platform which should screen us from prying eyes. I'm guessing the aliens didn't bother chasing us through here because they figured it would be easier to wait for us near the ship."

This thought is quite unnerving. The vegetation might hide us for a while, but we still have to find our lander. And if the aliens have the ship surrounded...

I would rather not complete that thought.

"Are you ready to travel, Sean?" Kartak asks, eyeing me.

Should I answer truthfully? If so, my response would be 'in about a year'. However, I want to get off this planet and away from danger as soon as possible. My muscles feel like they are barely going to function, but they'll just have to get the job done.

"Sure," I say, rising slowly to my feet. I don't collapse right back to the floor. So far, so good.

"Right, let's get up on that branch and survey the situation," Kartak says.

I hobble after him, trying to conserve some energy for all the climbing ahead. Not to mention the running, dodging, and – gulp – possible fighting.

Kartak and Sharden boost me through the opening. This branch, while still quite wide, is narrower than the one below. The wind also feels stronger. I keep to the very middle as I crawl away from the exit. Wiggs comes up next, followed by Sharden, and finally Kartak.

We head toward the landing pad. It is almost three yards thick, and appears to be smooth – no handholds or footholds. The others might be able to get up there, but I don't see any way I could possibly scale it.

"Okay, here's the plan," Kartak says, after examining the platform edge. "I will get down on all fours. Sean will climb onto my back and jump from there. Sharden, you and Wiggs will help boost him up."

I feel my mouth drop open. Does he really think this will work? It's more likely I'll break his back, or knock Wiggs and Sharden off the branch. I can't possibly get onto the platform.

"This isn't going to work," Sharden says.

"Yes, it will," Kartak replies firmly, getting down on his hands and knees.

Sharden looks at Wiggs. Wiggs shrugs. "I don't have any better ideas."

Sharden puffs out his breath. "Neither do I. Let's give it a try."

Wiggs helps me clamber onto Kartak's back. His skin slides back and forth, making it hard to keep my balance. Sharden slides into position. With Wiggs bracing me from one side, Sharden from the other, it helps stabilize me. Tossing my helmet onto the platform with a clatter, I bend my knees, and gather my strength.

"Okay. One, two, three!" With that I launch upward as far as I can go – which isn't far at all. I hear Sharden and Wiggs grunt as they try to boost me up a bit. I manage to grab the edge of the platform with my fingers. A pair of hands starts pushing on my rump – Kartak must have joined the effort. Soon I'm able to get my forearm onto the platform. I keep straining, and finally get my waist up against the edge. I lift my right leg up. My balance is precarious. There is a moment where I'm sure I'm about to plunge back to the branch. Then I manage to roll a bit, and finally my entire body is on the platform.

I lie here, appreciating the feel of a firm foundation under me. Incredible as it seems, I somehow managed to scale the side!

One after another, three helmets pop over the edge and bounce onto the platform, coming to a stop just inside the greenery. A mixture of scents assaults my nose as I wade into the vegetation after them: musty, oily, coppery, and something like the insides of a pumpkin. I quickly collect the helmets and set them within easy reach.

Sharden scrambles up next, and then Wiggs. They both turn and lie on their bellies, stretching over the edge of the platform to help Kartak up. My muscles tense as they start to slip forward...

"Sean, could you give us a hand?" Wiggs asks in a strained voice. At first I'm not sure what to do. After thinking for a second, I realize my weight can come in handy for once. Lowering ponderously to one knee, I push aside a couple of plant stalks and lie across their calves, anchoring their legs.

A minute later, it's over. We are all up.

A moment after that, I realize it's only beginning, as the pod of a nearby plant explodes. A shower of yellow powder rains down on us. Another pod explodes, and another. Through the foliage, I see a group of aliens similar to our captors. Most of them are aiming weapons at us. Kartak was right. They have simply waited for us to show up on the landing pad.

Several large insects swarm in and tackle one, and then another of the tentacled beings. But the rest of the aliens don't even hesitate; they just keep advancing, their weapons blazing.

"Quick, use this ship as cover," I say, diving behind the hull of an alien vessel. Kartak races over as several pods burst apart simultaneously.

I lean against the hull of the ship, wondering how we can possibly make it back to the lander. Something splashes against my cheek. This is wet, different from the dry powder of the pods. Looking up, I realize it's starting to rain. Great. Now the platform will be slippery, making it more difficult to run and dodge alien weapons.

"This ship isn't too far from the lander," Kartak says, peering around the hull to where the aliens are advancing. I'm amazed at his certainty. How can he possibly recall alien designs with such confidence? "The only problem is," Kartak continues. "The lander is in the other direction."

"Right, we need a diversion," Sharden says, after a brief pause. He seems to have something in mind. I see him reach into a pocket and pull something out: the multi-tool. "Get ready to run to the lander," he says, extracting the tool from its case.

Sharden strides to the far end of the alien vessel and peeks around the corner. After a moment, he turns and stabs the nearest pod with the multi-tool. It bursts apart with a loud pop. He stabs two more. Then several pods explode with a sizzling electrical discharge. At least some of the aliens have moved over to that side of the ship.

"Run!" Sharden shouts, putting his words into action as he barrels toward us, his face looking weird with its coating of yellow powder from the plants. I start sprinting as fast as my chubby legs can carry me, crashing through the vegetation.

Chaos reigns.

Pods are bursting, leaves are getting shredded, rain is drumming against my head, and I'm plowing through stalks and tangled vines. I can't see anything but thick vegetation.

"Here, Sean, right here!" Kartak shouts.

I twist around and see that he's angling to the left. Trying to change direction quickly, I slip on the rain-slick platform and plop to the ground. I'm sliding toward the edge of the landing pad. I grab at vines and plant stalks to halt my momentum. It takes several tense heartbeats, but I'm able to regain my feet and find traction. A second later, I crash through a final layer of vegetation, and then I'm at the lander.

The airlock hatch is already sliding smoothly open. There are two aliens lying unconscious on the ground just beyond the hatch. Kartak is amazing. I don't know how he was able to incapacitate them so quickly, especially taking them on alone without any weapon. I gaze wildly around, expecting to see tentacles, breathing slats, and cold, hard eyes surging toward us with weapons blazing. So far, there aren't any. But that won't last long.

"Get in, Sean!" Sharden bellows. I turn and see Wiggs stepping into the lander. Kartak is already in the airlock. The hatch is still opening, but it is wide enough for me to squeeze through. I slip in, with Sharden at my heels. As soon as he clears the opening, Sharden slaps the sensor. The hatch reverses direction.

I can hear grunting. The aliens are getting close. The hatch should seal before they get to it, but what if one of the aliens lunges forward and fires a weapon through the gap before it closes? The nasty discharge could kill us...

"Secure your helmets!" Kartak orders. His voice makes me jump. I stand for a moment, unable to process the words. "Hurry, Sean!" Kartak says.

My brain unfreezes, and I nod. Water trickles down my cheeks and tickles as it runs down my neck. I shake my head to free my hair of excess moisture – reminding me of Bo's Labrador, spraying us all with water every time it emerged from the Lavaca Bay, after retrieving a tennis ball Bo had thrown. I get lost in the memory for a moment, but movement around me jars it from my mind. Sharden and Wiggs are sealing their suits – that's right! I quickly lift up my helmet. As I set it in place, I wonder why Kartak wants us to put them on. He must want to expel as much of the alien atmosphere from the lander as possible.

Several long seconds later, the hatch clicks shut. "Everybody's helmet sealed?" Kartak asks. Getting three affirmatives, he starts the airlock cycle. Time seems to trudge slowly by. What if the aliens have more powerful weapons, weapons that can damage the lander? What if they are mustering right outside, ready to disable us? We need to lift off as quickly as possible!

The airlock doesn't cooperate. I gaze at the readout, waiting for the indicator light to switch from red to green. Surely the cycle must be finished by now. It never seemed to take this long before. The aliens are probably setting up their big guns, gazing at their targeting systems, lining up their shots. Any second, and they'll be ready to fire...

The light finally flashes to green. Kartak instantly hits the sensor and dashes toward the cockpit, unsealing his helmet as he runs. By the time I waddle to the flight deck and get my helmet off, his hands are flying across the control surfaces.

"Everyone strap in. This might get a bit bumpy," he says.

I take the seat behind him and secure my restraints. I'm not tall enough to see what's happening outside the viewport. What are the aliens up to?

I hear a sound to my right. Looking over, I see Sharden wiping yellow powder off his face. Next to him, Wiggs is pulling the upper part of his spacesuit down to his waist. His chest is bare. Ribs furrow the skin. His shoulder blades stick out sharply. His arms look like they might snap under the slightest bit of pressure.

The thrusters growl, drawing my attention away from Wiggs. The lander shakes and rattles. Electrical current arcs across the viewport; the aliens must be firing. The lander hops forward a few feet, and thumps back to the platform. Are the thrusters damaged?

"Hold on!" Kartak shouts. I feel the lander lift a bit. Kartak swings the nose around so that we are facing the edge of the platform. I hear a great rustling sound as we tear through the vegetation.

Then the lander drops.

CHAPTER 11

Wiggs

We plunge down, through a layer of clouds. Soon we leave the fluffy mass behind, and hurtle toward the planet surface. Kartak's hands work the control surfaces quickly but calmly. Details of the landscape start to emerge. Before long, I'm able to pick out different types of vegetation. The images sharpen as we draw closer. I grip my armrests, my eyes fixed on the planet surface rushing toward us.

Abruptly, I'm shoved back in my seat as the main drive kicks in. Kartak works the controls, trying to pull us out of our steep dive. The nose of the lander edges upward. We're nearing the tops of the more normal-sized trees that are scattered around the grassland. We'll go crashing through the treetops, and that will be the end of the lander. It will happen very soon now.

The nose of the lander inches upward, but it's still not enough. A few more seconds, and we will be tearing through trees and plowing into the ground. My heart thumps out its final beats. I brace myself for the impact...

It doesn't come. I hear a grinding screech as we skim the top branches of the trees, but Kartak has us leveled out. And now we're climbing.

A dreamy, pastel dusk settles across the sky. Everything looks peaceful. But it's deceptive. What will we see once we climb above the clouds? Will the air be swarming with ships waiting to shoot us down? If only I knew how to read the sensor display, I would have some idea of what's awaiting us.

Soon there's a uniform white outside the viewport. A second later, we punch through to clear sky. I strain my eyes, but don't see any sign of craft ahead of us. That doesn't mean anything. There could be dozens of ships behind us, or farther up in the atmosphere where I can't see. The lander starts to shudder every few seconds. Is this normal turbulence, or is some kind of weapon being fired at us?

Kartak changes the angle of ascent, and I briefly catch a glimpse of something. I'm not entirely certain, but it looks like a flaming rose. Seconds later, the lander shakes again. This isn't simply turbulence. We are under attack.

I'm so intent on the viewport, I barely notice my stomach do a funny flip. My body instantly feels lighter. I look down, and momentarily forget my fear. Wiggs's spacesuit has fallen to my waist: arms, chest, and stomach are exactly as I remember them. I'm back to being skinny!

Again the lander judders, jarring me from the joyful inspection of my true body. The sky has turned a deep purple. There is a spacecraft off to our right, angling toward us. Up ahead I see one of the space stations, with different craft arriving and departing from the giant structure. Kartak adjusts our vector, and I nod in understanding. He is trying to put the station and its traffic between us and our pursuers.

"*Aurora*, this is Kartak."

There is a pause. "*Aurora* here." It sounds like Johnson's voice.

"We ran into some trouble," Kartak says. "We've got some bogies on our tail."

Another pause. "Understood. Is there anything we can do to help?"

"Just be ready to jet out of here the moment we're aboard," Kartak says grimly.

"Acknowledged."

As the voice cuts off, I notice a flashing red light on the instrument panel. This is quickly followed by a buzzing wail. Kartak glances down and winces. "It's going to be close."

This is not an encouraging statement. I still can't see the *Aurora*. If we're already getting sirens and warning lights, I don't see how the lander can hold together.

Again the lander rocks violently. The interior lights blink off momentarily, and then flicker back on. There is a low moan coming from the back of the ship. Several new red lights appear on the instrument panel.

We edge past a huge vessel – maybe a freighter or a barge – and a smaller ship looms suddenly on our right, heading straight for us. Kartak angles sharply "down".

The alien vessel flashes past, almost close enough to scrape the paint off our hull. That ship's engines must leave some kind of wake, because the lander starts bouncing around like we're on a choppy sea. For a few tense seconds, Kartak's hands work feverishly across the controls.

Just as he's getting the lander back under control, two more flaming roses erupt, one to our left, the other almost directly ahead. The crooked-fingered scientist kicks the lander down and to the right – but the lander's not quite nimble enough. We catch the edge of an explosion. Spaceships and space stations wheel outside the viewport as the ship spins and bucks. I don't know how much more of this the lander can handle. I'm sure it's tough, but the ship is taking quite a beating. After all, it's not a military craft.

Eventually the lander ceases its whirling and rattling, although I still feel a bit woozy. Kartak angles up and to the left, skirting a thick arm of the space station, and suddenly the *Aurora* swings into view, close enough to fill most of the viewport. The landing bay hatch is open, and we're approaching fast… too fast, in my opinion.

A moment later, Kartak hits the nose thrusters. Our forward rush slows; we slip through the hatch; the far bulkhead zooms toward us; we decelerate smoothly and come to a hovering halt, a few feet short of the bay wall. Kartak nudges the forward thrusters. We slip back to the center of the bay. There's a little bump as the landing skids meet the deck, and then the engines start cycling down.

"Neatly done!" I say, impressed with the timing and skill of the landing.

"Thanks, Sean," Kartak says, smiling back at me. "I see you're back to normal."

"Yes. It feels great!" I say, smiling back.

The deck gives a lurch, throwing me against my harness. "We'd better see what the situation is out there," Kartak says, unstrapping his restraints and standing up.

"I could use a little help first," Wiggs says, moaning.

I look over at him. Wiggs is also back to normal. Arms as thick as both of my legs put together; stomach overflowing the seat; and legs... legs that are trapped in a spacesuit many sizes too small. There is pain on Wiggs's face, but he's trying to hide it.

"Just a moment!" Kartak says, and hurries to a locker at the back of the flight deck. He produces a pair of shears from an emergency kit. "Here Sharden, help me."

The suit is so tight against Wiggs's skin, it's hard for Kartak to get the shears in place. He wiggles them and works them until he has part of a blade under the fabric. Sharden holds the fabric while Kartak cuts. It takes several minutes to finish the first leg, which is bright red and has crease marks on it. Kartak then begins on the second leg. Wiggs's face – the patches I can see through all the hair – is pale. His eyes are shut, and he seems to be rather dazed.

The left leg is nearly a purple color by the time Kartak finishes cutting the suit away. He leans down and gazes closely at the limb, and then looks up at Sharden. "We need to get him to sickbay."

Sharden nods. "I'll get a hover platform." He jogs out of the cockpit. I hear the airlock hatch open and close.

"Is he going to be alright?" I ask, gazing at the big guy. He's slumped down in his chair.

"He'll be fine," Wiggs says, opening his eyes and giving me a pained wink. "They say when people lose a lot of weight, they tend to gain it back. They just don't usually gain it back this quickly."

I try to smile at his attempt at humor. It's hard, when I can see that he's suffering.

Sharden returns with a hover platform, along with Johnson. Sharden's face and hair are glistening. He must have taken a quick second to wash all of the yellow powder off before collecting the hover platform. Judging by the fact that we haven't been quarantined, Sharden must have neglected to mention that we had to take our helmets off on the planet.

The three adults help Wiggs onto the platform. They maneuver it out of the lander. I'm anxious to see what happens to my friend, but I have to change first. Holding up the giant suit as best I can, I waddle to the storage rack on the lander. My new suit is still hanging on the rack.

I quickly change, and hang Wiggs's suit up on the rack. My current spacesuit is bigger than my old one. It's not as easy to move around in, but I don't want to take the time to stop at my cabin for clothes.

By the time I reach sickbay, Wiggs has been transferred to a bed. All the others are crowded around. Kartak is giving everyone a rundown of what happened on the planet. I push my way between Hollins and Dad, to catch a glimpse of the big guy. The color in his legs is starting to return to normal. I breathe a sigh of relief. It looks like Wiggs will be okay.

Kartak reaches the point where he woke up a prisoner. The captain gives a loud exclamation, but he doesn't interrupt. A look of disgust passes over several faces when he tells them about the insects. A shiver runs down my spine at the memory.

"And then I managed to put a space station between us and the ships," Kartak says, concluding his story.

"Well, this explains one thing," Dad says. Everyone looks at him quizzically. "Why we can't find any familiar stars," he explains, as if it's perfectly obvious what he's referring to. "This 'fat planet', as Sean calls it. We obviously aren't back in our own universe."

His words take a moment to sink in. I see the reaction of those around me: the shoulders slumping a bit, the sighs, the downcast eyes. The excitement and anticipation of seeing Earth again has been stolen away.

"At least no one was injured," the captain says, breaking the mood. "Still, you weren't able to get any supplies. There aren't any more rocky planets in this system. It's going to be cutting it close to find another planetary system."

"We could try another part of this planet," Kartak suggests.

"It's too risky," the captain says. "Plus, we've been accelerating since fleeing the ships. It would take a while to bring us back around."

"Are there any potential systems nearby?" Kartak asks.

"The computer has located three systems," the captain answers. "We are aiming for the one that seems the likeliest candidate to have what we need." Turning to the rest of us, the captain says, "Now everyone out. Wiggs needs to rest."

I take one last look at Wiggs before allowing myself to be herded out the door. Now that I'm not concentrating on the conversation, I realize two things: I need to change, and I need to get some food. It's been two days since I last ate. It feels like it's been a week.

CHAPTER 12

Space Walk

When I get to my cabin, I rummage through the drawers. There aren't many choices. Selecting a pair of old shorts and a worn-out t-shirt, I make a mental note to add laundry to my list. The shirt hangs rather loosely from my shoulders, but it's better than the spacesuit. I lay the suit on my bed and head for the dining room.

The door swishes open. I'm surprised to see several people around the table: Kartak, Sharden, Dad, and the captain. Kartak and Sharden make sense; they've gone as long as I have without eating. Perhaps the captain wants further details of the planet.

There isn't much food, but I dish up a sizeable serving. Certainly the captain won't chew me out for taking so much, considering I haven't eaten in so long.

His eyes narrow when he sees my plate. "Sean," he growls, turning his attacking eyes to me. I was wrong. He *is* going to snap at me for taking such a large helping. "I just wanted to let you know that you again have permission to come to the bridge."

I almost choke on my lettuce. This is so completely unexpected, I don't know what to think or say. Somehow I get the sense that Sharden had something to do with the captain's decision. I don't understand it.

"Uh, thank you, sir," I say, finally finding my voice.

"Your condition must have been an interesting challenge," Dad puts in, his eyes twinkling.

I think back to being overweight: how my muscles and joints were constantly aching; how difficult it was to move and breathe. "Yes, it was," I admit. "I'm definitely glad to have my normal body back."

"I don't blame you," Dad says.

There is a bit of silence, broken only by the sounds of scraping food onto a fork and chewing. I see the captain open his mouth as if he's about to say something, but the whoosh of the door makes us all look around. Johnson rushes in, his forehead wrinkled in concern.

"I don't know what those alien weapons were," he says, "but they sure did a number on the *Aurora*. I have a list of items that need immediate attention. Some of them will require exterior work."

"To do that, we'll have to bring the ship to a full stop," Kartak says grimly.

"That's right," Johnson replies.

I can hear the captain huffing and puffing. He is clearly agitated by the news. "Very well," he confirms. "Bring us to a stop. I'd better get to the bridge. Kartak, I need your help. Sharden, you had better come too."

Kartak nods. Rising quickly from his chair, he grabs the lettuce remaining on his plate. "Can't afford to waste food," he explains.

Kartak munches on his lettuce as he exits behind Johnson and the captain. Sharden eyes the serving platters, as if he's thinking about following Kartak's example and taking some food for the road. After a moment's hesitation, he turns and follows the others out the hatch.

Once the hatch has closed behind him, Dad says, "Did you really see huge insects taking down an alien?"

I get the feeling he is trying to ease the tension. And to my amazement, I find that it works. The memory of the chase scene flashes through my mind. "Yep. It was quite a weird sight," I say.

"And you managed to find Wiggs and Kartak because of the smell?" he asks.

"That's right. For once it was a good thing that Wiggs has such a distinct odor," I say. "If it wasn't for that, we probably would never have found Wiggs and Kartak."

"That's just unbelievable," Dad says. He falls silent. I take advantage of this by stuffing food into my mouth.

Before long I hear the hatch open again. It's Kartak. He looks right at me and says, "Finish up and get your suit on. You're coming out with me.

"I'm done," I say, after swallowing my last bite and taking a swig of water. "I'll be down right after I clear the table."

"Very good," Kartak says. "I'll be waiting for you at the airlock."

As I clear away the table, I think about the repairs we will be making. What kind of damage did the alien weapons do to the *Aurora*? How bad is it? Will we get it fixed in time to make it to another planet before our supplies run out?

Kartak is suited up and waiting when I arrive at the lower airlock. Johnson and Sharden are there as well. Kartak and Johnson look weird, with bulky tools hanging randomly off of their suits as if some alien fungus has sprouted on them.

Johnson helps Sharden with his umbilical tether. Kartak helps me. Unease flutters through my stomach as I see the line snaking from my suit back to the reel. The last time I used a tether was on the dark planet. My back got shredded by an unseen alien. The pain is still fresh in my mind. I shouldn't have to worry about aliens out here, but I can't stop the nervous feeling the memory evokes.

"Remember. Always move slowly out there," Kartak says. "You won't have any weight, but you will still have mass. If you build up too much momentum, you won't be able to stop. It will break your grip on the ship. Take it nice and easy."

"Thanks for the reminder," I say, giving a short nod.

Sharden secures Johnson's tether, and Johnson secures Kartak's. The air cycles out of the airlock. Johnson hits the release, and the outer hatch slides open.

Outside there is blackness deeper than any on earth, sprinkled with the pinpricks of stars. Even after everything I've done, after all the things I have experienced on this trip, seeing the infinite reach of space outside the hatch still unnerves me. The thought of getting separated from the *Aurora* – floating off through the cold, lifeless vacuum – is a recurring nightmare that wakes me up in a cold sweat.

And now I have to face it. This is no dream. One false move, and it would be the last mistake of my life.

I step closer to the edge of the airlock. My heartbeat picks up. The only other times I've done spacewalks were at the tulip people's planet. There was a breathable atmosphere around me, and friendly aliens to help. Here, there is no such help.

The others launch from the ship. I quickly jump after them before I lose my nerve. There is a funny feeling as I leave the artificial gravity of the *Aurora*. I float for a bit, then come to a sharp halt and rebound back toward the ship. Spinning slowly around, I see that Kartak has a hold of my umbilical with one hand, while his other hand grasps a handhold on the exterior of the ship. I feel my face flush at such a stupid mistake. I was so focused on getting out of the ship, I forgot to grab a handhold.

Kartak releases my tether, and uses his free hand to snatch my arm. This is a good thing. I'm still spinning, and as I reach the *Aurora,* my back is turned to the hull. If Kartak didn't catch me, I would bounce off the side of the ship, and head back into space again. I quickly grab onto the same handhold that Kartak is using, and take a moment to catch my breath.

"You okay Sean?" he asks. I can hear the concern in his voice.

"Sorry, yeah," I say. "Just a rookie mistake."

"Don't worry about it," Kartak says. "We've all made them."

"Now that we're all here, can we get to work?" Sharden snaps.

"Yes. Follow me," Johnson says. He heads aft.

"You go ahead of me, Sean," Kartak says.

"Okay," I say, knowing he probably wants to keep an eye on me. I wait for Sharden to get a head start, then begin pulling myself along using the handholds.

On the inside, the *Aurora* feels small, and seems to get smaller by the day. Out here, next to the hull, it's different. The ship's belly stretches before me. Johnson, already far ahead, looks like an infant crawling on the side of a great blue whale.

As I work my way along the hull, I try to guess what is beneath me. I imagine I'm passing by Wiggs's cabin and approaching the science stations. My arms soon start to burn with the effort of pulling my body along.

Sharden and Johnson have stopped. When I finally reach a handhold next to them, I see why.

The breath catches in my throat. There are several areas where the hull is bubbled, as if the strong alloy has somehow been frozen in mid-boil. In other places, there are holes with twisted metal edges in the outer-shell of the hull. These look like alloy flower blossoms, beautiful but potentially deadly. I don't know how we are going to repair this kind of damage.

Sharden and Johnson bend over one of the holes and get to work. "You are going to be my partner, Sean," Kartak says. We'll start over here. Let me get it prepped."

I join him at the spot he has chosen, and watch him work. First, he pulls a small pair of power clamps from his belt. A cable unwinds behind them, keeping the clamps tethered to his suit. Kartak attaches the clamp to one of the jagged edges surrounding the puncture. One section of the clamp slowly extends, straightening the curled edge of the hull plate back into place.

"Looks like that's the best it can do," Kartak says after a couple of minutes. The clamp hasn't been able to straighten the strong alloy completely. Part of it still juts out.

Kartak releases the clamp and moves it to the next jagged edge. He works his way around the hole, using the clamp to straighten the edges as much as possible.

Next Kartak pulls a small pair of power shears away from his belt. He snips away the pieces of hull plating that still project out, like he's clipping giant hangnails.

When this is done, he takes a third tool from his belt. This tool has a long cylindrical handle with a disc at one end. I peer at it, wondering what its function is. Kartak touches one side of the disc to the rim of the hole, and moves it slowly upward. It takes me a while to realize the disc is rotating. It must be some kind of sander or file, to smooth the edges. After running this all the way around the rim of the puncture, Kartak leans back and returns the device to his belt.

"That should do it," he says with a sigh. "Help me with this."

He pulls a small machine away from his suit. A tether unspools behind it. "Grab this side," Kartak instructs, "and help me set it as flush to the hull as possible." We work together to get the device into position, with me holding one side and Kartak holding the other. "After I activate it, we must make sure it moves as evenly as possible along the rim of the puncture," Kartak explains. "The alloy this produces isn't nearly as strong as the plating of the hull, but we'll apply several layers of it. The patch should be good enough."

Kartak presses the power stud. After a few seconds, the machine starts to move slowly across the ripped hull, our hands guiding it firmly. I watch in wonder as the machine leaves behind a strip that looks like metal gauze. When it reaches the far side of the puncture, Kartak slides the device down a bit, and reverses its direction. Another strip is laid down, overlapping the first strip. Again Kartak reverses its direction. The device moves steadily forward, spinning its alloy web. It takes seven passes to cover up the gash. Kartak powers off the device, moves it back up to its original starting point, and we get to work on the next layer. This time the device moves up and down rather than side to side.

After applying a third layer (this one at a forty-five degree angle to the others), Kartak reels the device back to his belt. "That should do it," he says. "Let's get the next one."

I turn to follow him. My head comes up, searching for my next handhold. I see the black void all around me. The sight is as unnerving as ever. I quickly return my gaze to the hull and follow Kartak to the next rip.

When we've finished our fourth patch, Kartak straightens up and looks at me. "The weaver needs fresh slugs," he says, indicating the device we've been using to seal the holes. "It's time for a break anyway. Let's head back."

"Do you want me to lead?" I ask, turning to orient myself toward the airlock. The view is dizzying. It takes me a moment to collect myself. It's important to focus my eyes on the *Aurora's* hull. This helps a bit. Scanning ahead, I can't see the hatch from here. I use my tether to make my best guess as to where it's at.

"Yeah, go ahead," Kartak says.

I wiggle my fingers and shake my hands to get the blood flowing properly. I'm not looking forward to the burning of my arm and shoulder muscles, but it's best to get it over with. Grabbing my first handhold, I begin the long journey back across the hull.

———

The second and third shift go much like the first. It's strange that, even though I'm weightless, the work still leaves me exhausted.

We have inspected most of the outer hull. There are only a few punctures left to patch. These are portside near the bow, just forward of where the lounge viewport is. Kartak bends and snips and files down the jagged edges, and then I help him with the weaver.

That's it. The final hole has been patched. Sharden and Johnson are finishing up on a long furrow that didn't quite punch all the way through the outer hull. I watch them apply the last bit of the third layer. The patch is a lighter color than the hull, making it look like the *Aurora* has a long, jagged scar on her cheek.

"There, now the ship has a bit of character," Kartak says, as Sharden and Johnson straighten up.

"Just so long as she doesn't acquire too much more character," Johnson replies.

Kartak moves over to one of the areas where the hull has been bubbled by an alien weapon. He pulls himself down for a closer look. He pauses there for a moment, as if memorizing every detail of the hull. "I can't think of anything we can do for this," he says, looking up at the rest of us.

Johnson joins him. "I agree," he says after a moment. "We don't have anything that can straighten that out or strengthen it. We'll just have to hope it holds."

I don't like the sound of this. What if those areas have been weakened? What if they suddenly collapse, or flake off? There are eight of the bubbled areas total, and two of them are near the engines. If one of those spots collapses, what will it do to the engines? In my mind, I picture the *Aurora* bursting apart in a brilliant explosion. All of us dead before we know it.

"Let's get back inside," Kartak says, interrupting my ominous thoughts. "My stomach is telling me it's supper time."

I take one last look at the bubbled surface, knowing I won't forget the sight any time soon. Hopefully, it's not a ticking time bomb.

And this is when it happens.

My mind is too focused on the damage to the *Aurora*, rather than what it should be focused on: my hands. I reach for a handhold and come up short. My momentum pulls my other hand free, and suddenly I'm drifting. After all this time out helping with repairs, I've made that mistake you can't afford to make on a spacewalk. I have gotten careless.

My nightmares instantly pop into my mind. They seem destined to come true. I wave my hands wildly, trying to grab something, but the hull of the *Aurora* is already out of reach. Nobody is close enough to grab my arm, no one is able to grab my tether.

I try not to panic. They can winch my tether in, reeling me in like a great fish. It's no big deal. This is what the tether is for.

But knowing this doesn't help. The only thing I can see is the ship getting smaller, the infinite void growing larger. It is waiting to swallow me whole. My breathing comes in quick gasps.

"Relax, Sean," Kartak says calmly. "I'm almost to the airlock. We'll have you back shortly."

The words should soothe me, but for once Kartak's steady voice doesn't have its magic. I can't shake the images of my nightmares. Closing my eyes, I try to relax.

My mind drifts, thinking about the tulip people, Bo and Hoss, and Mom. Her smiling face appears before me. The details aren't sharp. I realize I'm beginning to forget her. My eyes bolt open in sudden anguish. The person I love the most, and I'm forgetting her.

My breathing starts to pick up its pace again. How long has it been since Kartak called? Shouldn't I be feeling the tug of the tether tightening? Why hasn't he called me again? If something has gone wrong...

"Sean, we're back in. It should be just a few more moments," Kartak says.

I remember how big the *Aurora* is from the outside. It would take them a while to get back to the airlock. My panic has simply made it seem like a long time. This helps me relax, even though the *Aurora* now looks like the size of a large bus. I'm surprised I haven't come to the end of my tether.

This thought sends me into panic mode again. Has my umbilical become detached from the winch? Has it snapped? It still isn't tightening. What are they waiting for?

"Sean, we're having some trouble with the winch," Kartak says. "We'll pull you in by hand instead."

My mouth is dry. I don't trust myself to speak. I remain silent as finally, I feel a little jerk. And another.

"That should do it," Kartak says. "We don't want to give you too much inertia, otherwise it will be hard to stop you when you get here."

That makes sense. Even so, it means I'm going to be drifting at a very slow pace – assuming I'm heading in the right direction in the first place. How do they know I'm not heading for an orbit around the *Aurora*? If that happens, my tether will wrap itself around the ship, getting shorter with each pass. Yes, I would eventually make it back that way. However, a sharp edge on the ship might slice through my umbilical – which would fling me out into space and leave me with only a small oxygen reserve – and the maneuver would cause me to gain speed and momentum. In the end I would probably smash into the side of the ship, breaking every bone in my body. I definitely want to avoid that.

I still don't fully trust my voice, but I have to make sure. "Kartak?" I say tentatively. My voice squeaks a bit, but it's not too bad.

"Yes, Sean?" Kartak replies.

"Are you sure I'm heading directly toward the *Aurora*? I don't feel like becoming a temporary moon," I explain.

"We are coiling your umbilical as you approach. If we see that you're going off on a tangent, we can give a tug to redirect you. We won't let you miss your mark," he promises.

"Maneuvering thrusters would sure be nice right now," I say.

"You haven't been trained to use them," Kartak responds. "Believe me, they would be much more dangerous than helpful to you. Don't worry, we've got you."

His confidence is reassuring. It also helps that the ship is noticeably larger. I lean my head back, close my eyes, and try to enjoy the ride.

When I open my eyes again, the *Aurora* fills most of my view. The problem is, the ship is also slightly below me. If I

112

continue on this vector, I will pass over the top of the ship. "Kartak," I say hurriedly.

"We're on it, Sean," he replies, as if reading my mind.

There is a jerk on the line. I suddenly start drifting "down" at an angle. The open door of the airlock looms before me. I see the others secured to handholds, reaching their arms out to catch me. Several seconds later, I feel their grip as they try to slow my momentum. I rebound off the rear of the airlock, hit the floor, and slide along the deck toward the open hatchway...

Twisting around, I manage to snag a handhold. I slow down with a jerk that hurts my shoulder and rips my fingers from the grip. My legs are outside the hatch; I'm drifting away again...

Sharden and Johnson lunge for me. Sharden manages to grab an arm. This makes my body spin quickly around and hit the wall of the airlock. Johnson manages to secure a grip on my leg, and it's all over. It wasn't pretty, it wasn't fun, but I'm back aboard the *Aurora*.

CHAPTER 13

The Request

Dad is the only person in the dining room when we arrive. "The others are finished eating," he explains. "But I wanted to wait for you."

Kartak tells him about the repairs as we serve ourselves. "The captain sounded pretty optimistic when I spoke to him," Kartak concludes. "Now that we're back underway, he feels we have a chance at making it to another planet."

"I wish I could share his optimism," Dad mutters as he takes a bite.

Kartak doesn't seem to hear him. Instead, he turns to me. "And speaking of planets, I don't think I have properly thanked you for rescuing me and Wiggs from the aliens. I hate to imagine what would've happened to us if you hadn't shown up."

"Don't mention it," I mutter, feeling my face go red. "I'm glad we could help."

"Enough of this talk," Sharden says, scowling. He seems to be reverting to his old crabby self again. I wish he would leave. It would be nice to finish eating in peace. "It's time to talk about the future. How can we conserve our resources, so that we can survive long enough to reach another planet?"

I look up, impressed. Apparently he isn't simply being ornery. Sharden is actually thinking about everyone's welfare.

"What Yates said back in sickbay got me thinking," Kartak replies.

"What did I say?" Dad asks.

"About us not being in our own universe," Kartak explains. "I believe we have been in three different universes, each with unique physical properties."

"I don't see how that helps us," Sharden says with a scowl.

"It's possible we have enough data to determine how the universe boundaries interact," Kartak explains. "If we can create an accurate enough model, it might help us recognize the boundary to our own universe."

There is silence. Everyone is pondering the enormity of this idea. Finally, Dad says, "I think it's worth a shot."

Sharden is silent for a while longer. Finally, he nods. "I agree. Let's get started right after supper."

As we eat, the scientists discuss different factors they will need in their model: gravity, temperature gradients, the variations we've encountered in electromagnetic radiation. I barely understand any of the conversation.

The meal comes to an end. Kartak calls the captain on the intercom, and explains the plan. Captain Sharta is dubious, but in the end he gives his approval. We move to engineering compartment 3B. This is where the holographic model will be created.

The scientists begin with the tulip people's universe. They pore over all of the data they collected, discussing how each little tidbit of information might affect the model. It's much too complicated for me. My mind starts drifting after the first five minutes. I don't want to leave, though. Even if I can't contribute, I want to be here, where the vital work is happening.

Two hours later, the scientists are still debating how the reverse-gravity might shape space in that universe. I hear the hatch whoosh open. Focused on the discussion, I don't look up right away. Sharden finishes the point he is trying to make. Only then do I look up, expecting to see the captain hovering over our shoulders, checking up on our work. Instead, I get a welcome surprise.

"You guys are so intense! I didn't want to interrupt your fine debate," Wiggs says, a big grin on his face.

"You're out of sickbay, and on your own two feet!" I exclaim, smiling at the sight of him.

"It does work a lot better than borrowing someone else's feet," Wiggs says, chuckling.

"How do you feel?" I ask, running my eyes up and down his legs. They seem to be back to their proper color.

"Heavy," he says. "Which is why I want to ask something of you. Would you mind stepping into the corridor for a moment?"

I nod. "Sure, I could use a bit of a break." Pushing back my chair, I follow Wiggs out the hatch, wondering what's on his mind.

The hatch slides shut behind me. Wiggs checks both ways down the corridor, evidently wanting to make sure we are alone. Then he locks gazes with me. There's a look in his eyes I can't quite place. Hesitation? Embarrassment?

He stands there, without speaking, for several seconds. When he does speak, his voice sounds a bit uncertain. "Sean, I need you to do me a huge favor."

What could this possibly be about? Certainly Wiggs hasn't done anything to be ashamed of. He's been in sickbay since we got back. Why is he being so mysterious? I try to sound encouraging when I answer, "Anything."

"I need you to be my workout partner. I know I'll lose weight because of our food rationing, but some exercise would help me shed a few extra pounds."

That's what this is all about? I almost laugh out loud at my wild speculation, but I know Wiggs would take it the wrong way. "I would love to help you out!" I say, excited at the chance to assist the big guy. "Down on the planet, I got a little taste of what your life is like. I wouldn't wish that on anyone. Let's get you into shape!" I say, holding out my hand.

Wiggs smiles. "It's a deal!" he says, gripping my hand in a firm shake.

"If you're up for it, we'll begin before lunch tomorrow," I say, thinking about what kind of exercises it would be best to start with.

"That sounds ice!" Wiggs says, looking positively buoyant. He definitely looks committed to this. Will he be just as committed several days from now, when his muscles and joints are aching?

"Have you heard about the project?" I ask, turning back toward the hatch.

"Yes, the captain mentioned it to me," Wiggs replies. "I'm eager to help out."

"I'm sure they'll be glad to have you," I say, as the hatch swishes open. I hold out my hand, and allow Wiggs to precede me through the hatchway. Possible exercise routines are still running through my head. It takes me a moment to see the holographic light. They have finally started on the model.

Kartak, Sharden, and Dad are bunched around the control panel. Kartak's crooked fingers work the control surfaces. Wiggs plops down in a seat next to Dad while I peek over Kartak's shoulder.

"I think these star clusters would create more gravimetric eddies in this area," Sharden says, pointing at the model. Kartak fiddles with the controls, and the hologram changes slightly.

"That still doesn't resolve this issue," Kartak says, pointing to the area in question.

"Let me take a look," Wiggs says, rolling his chair around and looking at the model from different angles. His forehead wrinkles as gazes at one area for a long moment. "This is good," he says. "Very good. I would never have thought of the interactions behaving like that." He arrives back at the control board, tilts his head back, cups his face in his hands, and closes his eyes. His pinkies rub back and forth along the ridge of his brow.

Suddenly, Wiggs sits up straight and his eyes pop open. "What if it looks something like this?" he says, taking over the model's controls. Everyone leans forward in silent anticipation.

Several minutes later, Wiggs says, "How does that look?" The other scientists examine the holographic projection.

"That's a possibility," Kartak says. "What do you guys think?"

"It doesn't look quite right," says Sharden. "But it's definitely closer than before."

"This isn't my area of expertise," Dad says. "I will leave it to your judgement."

"Let's sleep on it," Kartak suggests. "We'll come at it fresh in the morning."

"That sounds good to me," Sharden says. "I'm exhausted."

Kartak shuts down the holographic projector, and we file out. My body is tired from the work on the hull, and my mind is fried after listening to all of the complex conversations. When I get back to my cabin, I don't even bother undressing. I'm asleep in an instant.

———

After breakfast, Wiggs helps model the universes. I check in a couple of times, to see how the work is progressing. They are still working out different challenges of the tulip people's universe. The reverse-gravity is a headache. Every time the scientists come up with a theory that fixes one problem, it creates several others.

"I need a break," Wiggs says in the mid-morning. "Are you ready?"

"You bet," I say.

"Is there something I can help with?" Kartak asks, as Wiggs pulls himself to his feet.

"No, we can handle it," I reply quickly.

Kartak must understand something in my expression. He doesn't press the point. Smiling, he says, "Okay, have fun. We'll see you later."

Wiggs keeps up a constant stream of chatter as we walk. He is either super-excited, or super-nervous about the workouts. I can't tell which.

The gym is humid. The equipment has been scrunched into one corner. Large vats take up the remaining space – we've converted more than half of the gym into hydroponics, in order to increase our food supply.

"This humidity is sure going to make the workouts fun," Wiggs mutters, as he weaves his way through the vats.

"It'll be fine," I say, trying to put as much enthusiasm into my voice as possible. "Right, it looks like we'll need to shift equipment around between stations. We're going to start with the ground-bikes, so let's free up some space around them."

We clear an area, and then climb onto the ground-bikes. I call up the easiest level on both of them. The holographic view shows us starting off on level ground. A few yards down the trail, there is a slight uphill gradient, before leveling off again as it enters a forest. We wind between giant trees.

Within a minute, Wiggs is wheezing and his face is red.

"Do you need to stop for a bit?" I ask him, concerned that he might pass out on me.

"I've got this," he manages to strangle out.

We clatter across a wooden bridge and up another incline. Then around a bend and into a meadow. A deer is grazing to the right. It looks up and watches us warily as we pass.

The chronometer reaches five minutes. Wiggs's face is nearly purple. "Time for a break!" I say, bringing my ground-bike to a halt by a stony outcrop. Wiggs doubles over, panting heavily. "Let's walk around for a bit, and then try some more."

It takes him a great deal of effort to heave his body off the seat. As he walks, he holds onto the rims of vats, or leans into the wall. After three slow circuits of the room, Wiggs's breathing is almost back to its normal wheeze, and he can walk without support.

"I'm ready for another round," he croaks, clambering back onto his ground-bike. I want to object; it wouldn't do Wiggs any good to have a heart attack. But he is already starting up again.

We break after four minutes this time. Wiggs staggers once around the room, and then walks from vat to vat, checking to make sure everything is functioning properly. He takes an especially long time on the final vat, even though all of the readouts are normal.

"Right, one more set," he says finally, visibly bracing himself.

We return to the ground-bikes and get started. Wiggs pushes himself for another four minutes. After stopping, he sits slumped on his seat, looking like a great sagging jack-o-lantern.

"Tell me I can do this," the big guy says, so faintly I barely hear him.

"You can do this," I reply. "I won't let you down."

Wiggs huffs and puffs a bit longer and then heaves himself off his seat. "I need to shower and change before lunch," he says, gripping his shirt. It is soaked through and clings tightly to his skin.

"It's just a little sweat," I say, eyeing my own drenched shirt. Seeing his expression, I hastily say, "Yes, yes, yes. Of course I'm going to shower too."

Wiggs nods wearily. Before he hits the hatch sensor, the big guy turns to me and says, "Now that I can breathe, my body actually feels pretty good."

"I told you you could do this," I say, stepping through the hatchway. I don't mention the fact that tomorrow, his body almost certainly won't be feeling good. I'm quite positive he knows this already.

The quick shower feels good. I am no longer sweaty. And now that I've done laundry, I actually have clean clothes to put on.

Most of the others are already gathered when I arrive at the dining hall. As I sit down, Wiggs serves me a thin slice of meat, two stalks of broccoli, and a salad made out of three lettuce leaves, and a few sprigs of some herb. I take my time chewing the food, thinking that perhaps if I make the meal last longer, I can trick my stomach into thinking it's receiving more food than it actually is.

By the time I finish, the dishes have been cleared and most of the others have left. I quickly take my plate to the kitchen, place it in the washer, start the cycle, and join the design team.

Ten minutes into the discussion, the captain strides in, followed by Marcum. "Right, what have you got for me?" he asks, his eyes fixed on the holographic model.

"We aren't as far along as I had hoped," Kartak admits to him. "But we should be close to finishing the first universe."

The captain inspects the model from every angle. After about five minutes, he turns to Marcum. "What do you think?" he asks.

Marcum scrutinizes the model for several more minutes, his brow furrowed. Eventually, he looks at the captain. "It's like nothing I've ever seen before," he says. "This isn't my realm of expertise. We'll just have to trust them."

Captain Sharta turns to Kartak. "How much longer do you think it will take to finish all three universes?"

"The gravity in the other two universes is more similar to ours, so the second and third model shouldn't take as long," he says, cracking his knuckles as he speaks. "As long as there aren't any hiccups, I would say three or four more days."

The captain sniffs. Evidently, this is longer than he was expecting. "Very well," he says at last. "If that's what it takes to make sure this blooming thing works, then that's what we'll do. Keep me up to date on your progress."

"Yes sir," Kartak says.

"Ok, Marcum, now to the auxiliary pumps," the captain says. He turns on his heel and vanishes out the hatch. Marcum follows at a slower pace.

"Well, gentlemen, we have four days to get this all mapped out," Kartak says, hunching his shoulders and reaching for the control panel.

CHAPTER 14

The Dream Team

Three days turns to four, four stretch into five. The captain visits more frequently. I'm not sure about the others, but it definitely makes me nervous knowing he's hovering silently in the background, his attacking eyes following every move we make.

I finish breakfast on the seventh day, and head over to engineering compartment 3B. The rest of the team is already here, hunched around the control panel. Not wanting to interrupt their thoughts, I stand quietly by the hatch. Before long, Kartak straightens up and rubs his eyes.

"I believe that's it," he says wearily.

"I agree," Sharden says.

A tingling excitement shivers through me. "It's ready?" I ask.

Kartak turns toward me and grins. "We can start the search as soon as we get the captain's seal of approval. Would you do the honors?" he says, motioning toward the comm board.

"Of course!" I reply. As I head to the comm system, I say, "Computer, where is Captain Sharta?"

"Captain Sharta is in main engineering," the computer replies.

I activate the comm and hit the code for main engineering.

"What is it?" I recognize Marcum's voice.

"This is Sean. I would like to talk to the captain."

A moment later, the captain's voice booms through the room. "What is it, Sean? Make it quick. I'm busy!"

"S… Sir." I try to steel my nerves, but I still stammer. "The universe model is ready."

There is a short pause. I picture the look on the captain's face as he processes this piece of information. Then the captain's voice booms out again. "That's great news! Tell Kartak I will be there as soon as I'm finished here."

"Yes s – " I start to reply, but realize he has already cut the transmission at his end.

Only a few seconds later, the captain barrels through the hatchway. His eyes are bright, his face flushed with excitement.

"Here it is," Kartak says, moving his arm to indicate the holographic model.

The captain immediately starts scrutinizing the design. Before long, Marcum strolls through the hatchway and joins the captain. Every few minutes, he manipulates the controls of the projector. They seem to be taking much longer than necessary to examine the design. Do they see a flaw that we didn't catch?

Finally, the captain turns his gaze on Marcum. The engineer gives a nod. Captain Sharta grunts and turns to Kartak. "This looks good. You have my permission to get started on it right away."

These words seem to release the tension in the room. Dad thumps Kartak on the back, Sharden mutters something to the crooked-fingered scientist, and Wiggs flashes me a big grin. I grin back. A feeling of anticipation tingles up inside.

"Well done, everyone!" the captain booms, and then heads out the hatch.

"Let's get the sensors working on this right away," Kartak says. "We've done great so far, but the real work is still ahead."

I wait while the others clear out. Wiggs lingers in the hatchway, keeping an eye on the group moving up the hallway. Once everyone else is out of earshot, he says, "They can do without me for a bit. Are you ready for another workout session?"

There's nothing I can do to prepare the sensors. Exercising will help keep me occupied. "You bet," I reply. I've been impressed by Wiggs's commitment. The sessions have been brutal on him, but he keeps at it doggedly.

"I have a bit of a surprise for you," he says mysteriously. "I'll meet you in the gym."

I glance at his face, trying to get some clue as to what the surprise may be. His eyes are twinkling, and his goatee twitches as he smiles. But there is no hint in his face that I can see.

He heads toward his quarters. I turn right and head straight for the gym, wondering how the work on the sensors is going. With Kartak in charge, I'm confident everything will go smoothly. Since it will be a few minutes until Wiggs gets here, I use the time to move equipment around, so that we can get started on our first set as soon as he arrives.

I get everything ready. Wiggs still isn't here. I fiddle with some of the solutions on the vats, wondering if he's delaying on purpose to build up the suspense for his surprise. If so, it's working. My curiosity is growing by the second.

It is another five minutes before Wiggs comes huffing and puffing into the room. He is holding something in his hands. As he gets closer, I'm able to see the device better. It looks like a holographic projector, but slightly different. Wiggs doesn't say anything – he can tell that I'm curious, and he evidently wants to stoke that curiosity even further.

The big guy reaches the center of the room, slides the covering half-way across the top of a vat, and places his device on the level surface. After tinkering with it for a few moments, he stands up with a satisfied grunt. The device emits a beam, which produces a large rectangle of light on the far wall.

"This is a video projector," Wiggs explains at last. "It produces two-dimensional images. It will give us something to keep our minds occupied while we work out. Hopefully, this will prevent me from thinking too much about how terrible my body is feeling. Plus, I figure it's time to introduce you to some classics."

He rubs his hands together and grins. "You are in for a huge treat. Here I have three of the greatest shows ever made. I know the quality of the images will be a lot different from what you're used to, but you're going to love it!"

He fiddles with the device a bit more. "There, that should do it," he says, stepping back. "Now, to get started with our exercises."

As we begin our lower-body workout, there is a terribly loud noise. My head whips up and my heart starts thudding. There's been another explosion! Are the others all right?

A moment later, I realize that the sound actually came from the projector. It's only a part of the soundtrack. Feeling foolish, I relax back into my workout. Hopefully Wiggs didn't notice how much the soundtrack startled me.

The first images appear. They are flat and dull and unrealistic. Something that I assume is supposed to be a spaceship enters the screen, accompanied by sounds. Why would there be sound like this in the vacuum of space? It doesn't make any sense.

And then I see IT. A second ship comes. And comes. And comes. It is enormous. I forget all about the quality of the images, or the fact that there are sound effects in the vacuum of space, and I get lost in the story.

After finishing our workout, Wiggs goes to pause the video. "Wait. Let's finish it!" I say. Wiggs beams at me and nods. We settle onto the deck. Even though I know it isn't real, I still get chills when I watch the space battles. They remind me of my nightmares, drifting off into space alone.

The end credits start to roll. The show is over, but I want it to keep going.

"Let's watch the next one!" I say.

"I want to save it for our workouts, remember?" Wiggs says, using a vat to pull himself to his feet.

"Well, I say there's no time like the present to begin our next workout," I reply. I know Wiggs is anxious to show me the vids. It shouldn't take much to persuade him.

Wiggs chuckles. "I suppose we have time for one more before supper," he says. After switching to the second vid, we move the gym equipment around for our next series. I'm just hauling the final exercise machine into place when I hear the hatch open. It's Sharden.

"Look at what we have here. It's the dream team," he says snidely. "I'm sure you won't mind if I exercise for a bit."

Frankly, I do mind, but I don't voice the thought. Instead, I shrug my shoulders and turn back to Wiggs. "Would you give me a hand with this?" With his help, I get the piece of equipment into place. Gazing around, I note the layout of equipment. "It looks like everything's ready," I say. "Let's start that next vid!"

Wiggs activates the device, and we get started on our exercises. Again I hear the loud bang at the beginning of the show. I had forgotten about that. It startles me a bit, but I recover quickly. I can't say the same for Sharden. He gives a yelp, and flinches as if he thinks he's under attack. "What's that racket!" he demands.

"It's an old 2-D vid," Wiggs explains. "Sean and I are watching the series."

Sharden grumbles and glowers at Wiggs. Sneaking a peek at him between sets, though, I have to hide a smile. The grouchy scientist is watching just as intently as we are.

Once the workout is done, we settle to the floor to finish the vid. Even Sharden stays, although he grumbles about how it's 'such a waste of time'.

The second vid comes to an end. Wiggs switches off the projector. I continue to sit here for a moment, in awe of what I've just seen.

"Unbelievable," Sharden says. I glance over at the scientist, wondering what he's going to complain about this time. Once more, he surprises me. Fixing his eyes on my face, he asks, "Can you believe that was his father?"

It takes me a moment to get over my shock at this attitude from Sharden. Perhaps he truly is starting to change. I shake my head. "Like you said, it's unbelievable."

Looking at Wiggs, Sharden says, "Did I hear you right? Is there one more vid in this series?"

Wiggs nods. "There's a rumor that more of them were made, but I've only been able to find these three."

"Would you do me a favor?" Sharden asks. Seeing Wiggs's quizzical look, he says, "Will you wait until I'm available to watch the third one? I want to see how it ends."

I can see my shock at this request reflected in Wiggs's face. Perhaps Sharden is tired of not getting along with people. He seems to be making an effort to be a part of the group. "Sure thing," Wiggs stutters, once he has recovered a bit. "And believe me, you're going to love the finale!"

CHAPTER 15

Decision

I jerk awake, breathing heavily. A piercing alarm is blaring. Panicked, I try to rise from my bunk. Because I'm still half-asleep, I miscalculate where the edge of the bunk is and slide too far. Thump! I find the deck the hard way.

Rubbing my left hip, I hurriedly pull on a t-shirt and head out. My cabin door slides open. The siren is even louder in the corridor. Covering my ears, I jog to the bridge, wondering what catastrophe awaits us.

As I enter the bridge, I note that almost everyone seems to be here. But then I forget all about that as my eyes dart to the viewport. I stand paralyzed, staring out the transparent canopy. Dozens, maybe hundreds, of rocks fill the view. Most of them are small, barely visible in the dim light of the distant star, and the running lights of the *Aurora*. A few of them are the size of a cantaloupe. One flashes by that's as big as a hopper.

The shields are handling most of the hits… so far. Even so, I wince as an occasional ping tells me an asteroid has gotten through.

"Computer, silence siren!" the captain yells above the piercing wail. Immediately, it cuts off. A heavy silence descends upon the bridge as we stare at our doom.

"Computer, have you found a vector out of this mess?" Johnson asks. His voice sounds calm, but his hands are squeezing the armrests of his chair. Even the usually unflappable first officer is nervous.

"Negative. There is no vector with a consistently lower concentration of asteroids. It is unclear how far the field extends."

"So we don't know whether we're going across the width, or straight down the gullet of the beast," the captain mutters. "Johnson, take us –"

His words are drowned out by a loud BOOM. I'm thrown from my feet. I fly toward the viewport, wondering if this is the end.

As I hit the control panel, the computer blares out, "Warning! Hull breach in sector two. The sector has been sealed off. The seal will not hold."

The computer's statement jars my nerves. If I remember correctly, engineering compartment 3B is in sector two. Before I lay down for my nap, Kartak and Sharden were headed there to make some tweaks to the universe model. My throat tightens at the thought. "Captain, are Kartak and Sharden still in the engineering compartment?"

The captain doesn't answer, but the look on his face tells me all I need to know. My stomach plummets. I reach for the back of a chair to steady myself. I can't imagine them dead. My mind turns over the situation, trying to find some glimmer of hope. Perhaps the breach is in one of the other compartments of the sector. If that's true, Kartak and Sharden may be okay.

After a short pause, the captain says, "Johnson and Yates, suit up and check sector two. If there is any way to extract Kartak and Sharden, you will get them out. But remember, the safety of the ship is your first concern."

Johnson opens a locker on the starboard side of the bridge. He hands an emergency pressure suit to my dad, and pulls one out for himself. Waph and Hollins cross the bridge to help them.

I can't stop myself. Even though I know what the captain's response will be, I have to say it. The seal on the sector isn't going to hold. Every second counts. "Sir, there may not be time to suit up."

"I'm not going to send anyone in without a suit," the captain bellows. "It's bad enough having two men in danger. I'm not going to risk additional lives without taking precautions!"

The captain is right. I also know that I'm right. We need to get Kartak and Sharden out *now*. There is no doubt, no second-guessing in my mind. The captain sits down in the piloting chair, his eyes on the control board. Nobody seems to be paying any attention to me. I slip out the hatch and jog to sector two.

The entire sector is sealed off by a bulkhead door. However, each compartment has an individual hatch that also seals in the event of a breach. I quickly check a status screen. According to the display, the atmosphere is at full-pressure on the other side of the door.

"Computer, unseal bulkhead door on sector two," I say, mentally preparing myself for what I might see.

"Authorization required to unseal the hatch," the computer replies.

This stymies me. Only the crew members have such authorization. But I'm desperate. I have to try something. "Computer, there is atmosphere beyond the hatch. The secondary hatches are all sealed. Kartak and Sharden are in danger. Now open this door right now!"

Nothing happens for about ten seconds. There is no way this will work. The computer won't respond to reason. It will simply follow its programming. What could possibly be taking it so long?

I hear a click and see the light above the bulkhead door change color. A second later, the door slides to the side.

Hardly believing my luck, I rush to compartment 3B. The status screen indicates there is atmosphere beyond the hatch. A weight lifts from my chest. Kartak and Sharden could still be alive!

"Computer, open hatch to engineering compartment 3B," I say. This time there is no hesitation. The hatch slides open, and I step into the near-darkness.

It takes my eyes several moments to adjust to the dim glow of the emergency lights. A horror of destruction is slowly revealed: buckled plating; twisted and fallen support beams; mangled conduits. Most horrifying of all, though, is the view to my right: there are tiny dots of light in a sable sea. The glimmer of the distant stars shimmers slightly through the force field containing the breach. Tearing my eyes from the petrifying sight, I search for my comrades.

I spot Sharden first. He is lying on the deck to my left, trapped by a twisted girder. Another couple of steps brings Kartak into view. He is pinned to the back wall by a piece of machinery. He is farthest away, and thus in the most danger. I step around a wrecked computer station. Now I'm close enough to see Kartak more clearly. He is calmly attempting to work himself free.

"I'm okay," he says. "Help Sharden first."

I hesitate a moment. Kartak is in more danger. And Sharden. Well, I haven't entirely gotten over the way he used to treat me. "We'll get you out, and then –"

"There's no time to argue, Sean!" Kartak says emphatically. I see the look in his eyes. There is no way he is going to budge. And he's right. We can't afford to waste a single second.

"Okay, I'll be right back," I promise, and reluctantly turn away from the crooked-fingered scientist.

When I reach Sharden, I see that it's his left ankle that's trapped. The girder looks heavy. "We'll have to do this together," I tell him. I get a good grip on the girder with both of my hands. "Ready?" I ask.

"Just get on with it," Sharden replies in a strained voice.

"On three. One, two, three." I heave with all of my might. Sharden grunts and wiggles his foot. It slips out an inch or so. I close my eyes and continue to strain.

"Almost there," Sharden says. I open my eyes. A second later, his foot slips free. I let go of the girder and stand, with my hands on my knees, gulping in air.

"Can you stand?" I finally manage to gasp.

"I'll need some support," Sharden replies. He moans in pain as he tries to rise. I put his left arm around my shoulders, and lead him to the hatch. The grouchy scientist hobbles along beside me.

It's too dangerous to leave him outside this compartment. I must get him all the way out of the sector. It is a longer trip, but necessary if the seal gives out. We reach the corridor. Every second is precious. Even so, I pause long enough to help Sharden slide to the deck. He needs medical attention, but I must get Kartak out first.

I dash back to the compartment. Kartak is still trying to wiggle out from behind the machinery that has him pinned. It looks heavy. I don't know how I can possibly help, but I start trying to tug it away from Kartak.

A loud rattle followed by an ominous hum makes me look up. The force field sealing the hull breach seems to shimmer and flicker, as if it's about to die. If it goes, Kartak and I are dead.

I can't worry about that right now. Turning my back on the terrifying sight, I redouble my effort with the machinery. I have to get Kartak out!

"The seal is going to collapse," Kartak says. His voice is more strained than I have ever heard it. "Leave me. Go. Get out!"

I ignore him. I'm not going to leave him here. Not while there's still hope.

The machinery moves a bit. More hands grab next to mine. Johnson has arrived. The machinery gives a bit more, and Kartak is able to slide out. He collapses to the floor.

Johnson grabs one armpit, I grab the other. We haul Kartak around overturned tables and equipment. The hum of the containment screen rises in pitch and intensity. I know it's only a matter of seconds before it fails completely. I try to speed up, but there's just too much debris in the way. Kicking aside an overturned diagnostic table, I strain in the most important tug-of-war of my life.

We reach the hatch. I edge through, with Johnson right behind me. We heave with all of our might to get Kartak out of the compartment. I hear a loud squeal from the containment field.

The airtight door slams down.

Screaming. I will never forget the sound. It stirs up horror and anguish and hopelessness in my soul. Kartak's screams give life to his agony.

His legs have been cut clean off by the airtight door. I hear shouts and other confused noises. My mind doesn't seem to be working very well. There is a pool of red on the deck. Something deep inside my brain is unsettled by the sight, but I can't figure out why. After several seconds, I realize it's blood. There's a lot of it. I see a flurry of movement, but it takes my brain a while to figure out what is happening. Eventually, I realize Johnson has snatched a tool from his belt, and is doing something to Kartak's legs. The flow of blood slows, and then stops.

Someone pushes me gently out of the way and takes my place. He helps Johnson haul Kartak away from the door. I stand, looking at the crooked-fingered scientist in shock. Kartak is free of the hatch, free of the compartment – but it has cost him his legs.

Johnson and Dad rush him to sickbay. I stumble after them in a daze. It's my fault this has happened to Kartak. If I had freed him first, he would have his legs.

The sickbay hatch opens on a grim scene. Emergency lighting flickers across Johnson's face as he hoists Kartak onto a bed. He tries to activate the diagnostic scanner. Nothing happens. 'Insufficient power' flashes across the screen.

Johnson works quickly. He exposes wiring from several emergency lights, and cross-connects them to the diagnostic scanner. Johnson activates the scanner again. It gives a feeble warble.

"I don't think we'll have full function, but perhaps it will be enough," Johnson says grimly.

The hatch opens and the captain hurries in. His eyes lock onto mine. I can't quite make out his expression in the dim light, but I imagine a scorpion that has just had its tail trod on might have a similar look on its face. I'm certain the captain knows exactly what I did. I brace myself for a rebuke or a tirade. The captain holds my gaze a moment longer. Then his body seems to sink back to its normal posture. He turns to Johnson and asks, "How are they?"

"Sharden's wounds are minor," the first officer replies. "Kartak has lost his legs. I'm not sure if sickbay can give him the level of care he needs."

"Wiggs and Yates, you take over for Johnson. Do everything you can for him." Turning to his first officer, the captain says, "I need you on the bridge."

"Yes, sir," Johnson replies. "But first, I would recommend that everyone get into spacesuits. If Marcum doesn't get the environmental systems back to full strength, we may need them. Also, if there is another breach, we would be better prepared to deal with it."

Captain Sharta nods. "Very well. Everyone go suit up. Johnson, I want you on the bridge."

"Yes, captain," Johnson replies.

The captain and scientists turn toward the door. I'm about to follow when I feel a hand on my shoulder. "Sean, just a little reminder," Johnson says. "If we have to seal up our suits, then make sure you don't push your oxygen levels too far. We might have to recharge the bottles manually, and that takes a lot longer than doing it automatically. When your oxygen level drops below sixty percent, start recharging your bottles."

"I understand," I say, thankful that he has thought of this. I haven't had as much training for these kinds of scenarios as the adults have. I need all the pointers I can get.

Johnson nods and releases my shoulder. "Also, that was a very foolish thing you did, rushing to help Kartak and Sharden without suiting up. Brave, but foolish."

"We wouldn't have gotten them out if I hadn't," I say defensively.

"I know," he says softly. "Sometimes we need to be a little foolish."

This statement causes something to click in my brain. "It was you," I say. "You were the one who gave the authorization to override the bulkhead door."

Johnson nods. "I knew that you were going to try to help them. When the computer said there was atmosphere in the section, I decided to let you try. It was well done."

"But Kartak has lost his legs. It's all my fault."

"Kartak knows the risks of the job," Johnson says gently. "He understands that you did the very best you could for him. No doubt he will still find a way to do ten thousand different jobs better than anyone else." His voice turns a bit stern as he says, "Now, go get your suit on."

"Yes sir," I reply, and walk briskly to the hatch. Somehow, Johnson's little quip about Kartak eases some of my guilt.

Thoughts of Kartak fill my mind as I make my way to the lower level. He must be in unbearable pain. Will he survive these next few hours?

Wiggs, Hollins, and Marcum are already in the rack room when I arrive. Marcum has his suit on. He is adjusting his gloves as I enter.

"I'm going to help Johnson," he says, turning toward the hatch. "Hollins, I want you up there as soon as you're ready."

"Got it," Hollins replies.

Marcum gives me a nod as he exits. He is going up to help Johnson. A sudden thought breaks through my daze. Asteroids! In my concern over Kartak, I've forgotten what caused all this. We are still in the asteroid field. Any second could be our last.

I hurriedly grab my suit and start pulling it on. I check to make sure the seals are tight, check my oxygen and battery level, and then follow Hollins out the hatch.

The captain, Johnson, and Marcum are already on the bridge when we arrive. Johnson is seated at his station, his hands sliding smoothly across the control surfaces. "Number three starboard thruster is down," he announces softly, as I strap down. "Number one forward thruster firing at forty percent."

The captain motions Hollins to the sensor station. The scientist settles into the indicated seat, and starts poring over the data.

A small asteroid flashes into the *Aurora's* lights, bounces off the deflector screen, and slips silently into the night of space. A larger asteroid looms into view on our left, cutting across our path. I grip the armrests of my chair as Johnson maneuvers up and over the obstacle. The ship bounces as the asteroid punches into the deflector shield. I close my eyes, waiting for the impact. The ship wobbles like a leaf in gusty wind. It takes Johnson a few seconds to regain control.

Opening my eyes, I see that the viewport is clear. I relax my fingers once I realize the rock isn't going to be giving the *Aurora* any new scars. The miss was too close for my comfort.

"The asteroid density is definitely decreasing," Hollins announces several minutes later. "We should be near the edge of the field."

"Excellent!" Captain Sharta booms, pushing himself up straighter in his chair. "Great work Johnson!"

The first officer gives a brief nod. The dark skin of his hands stands out starkly against the lights of the control board. His focused gaze shifts between the viewport and sensor display in front of him.

"Maneuver positive five degrees y-axis," Hollins says. Johnson makes the necessary adjustment in the vector. Hollins lets out a breath. "That should do it," he says. "The scopes are clear for a hundred miles."

"Johnson and Hollins, continue to keep a sharp lookout for any rogues," the captain says. "Marcum, start a systems' check.

"It's time to see exactly what kind of shape the ship is in."

CHAPTER 16

Adrift

Darkness. Cold. The ship has lost power. The *Aurora* has limped out of the asteroid belt under Johnson's skilled guidance. Now we are drifting through space. The end is near.

Marcum has redirected most of the emergency power to sickbay, in order to stabilize Kartak's condition. Everywhere else on the ship, there is just enough energy to keep our suits charged. We are living in our spacesuits for warmth. We can't waste power on our suits' lamps, except when absolutely necessary. The best place to be right now is sickbay, where there is at least a faint glow to see by. But every second I spend in sickbay reminds me of the choice I made. The thought makes me sick to my stomach.

Standing by Kartak's bed, I gaze at his face, a contorted mask in the shadow-lit dusk. This is my fault. We are all going to die anyway. There is no way Marcum will be able to restore enough power to get us anywhere. The only thing I've accomplished by pulling Kartak out of that compartment, is to cause him unbearable agony, rather than letting him have a quick death.

"I'm so sorry," I mumble, not even sure if he can hear me. I've spoken these words to him often in the past few days. My throat is raw. My eyes sting. These are tiny islands of pain, compared to what he must be feeling. I wish there was some way I could undo this. If I could go back to that point in time, where I turned away from Kartak and toward Sharden...

I shake my head. The decision has been made. It was a terrible one. And it can't be reversed. I should never be trusted with any important decisions. I'm sure to mess them up.

"Sean, come away," a voice says gently from behind me.

I ignore him. Doesn't he understand? I have to stand by Kartak's side. I have to watch his pain. There is no way for me to shrink away from it.

There is the slight pressure of a hand on my shoulder. "Sean –"

"Leave me alone!" I shout, shrugging off the hand and moving closer to Kartak's head, away from my dad.

"Leave him alone, Yates," says Wiggs. The big guy seems to understand. He has stood by my side these past several days, mostly in silence, understanding that I don't feel like chit-chat.

"It's time to clear the room," the captain announces loudly over the spacesuit radio. "Kartak needs to rest."

I don't want to leave. My place is by Kartak's side. I know, though, that upsetting the captain won't get me anywhere. I follow Wiggs into the corridor. The sickbay doors slide shut behind us. We are left in absolute darkness. As dark as the bubble rides on the fat planet. As black as the dark planet.

I find the corridor wall with my left hand, and feel my way toward the lounge. There isn't any light in the lounge, but at least there are stars outside the viewport. It's nice to be able to see *something*.

I count hatchways as I pass. Reaching the correct one, I manually pump the hatch open. Wiggs follows me into the lounge. We leave the hatch open. I take a seat in the front row. He settles onto a nearby couch.

"Amazing," I say after a few minutes, speaking more to myself than to Wiggs.

"What's that?" he asks, wheezing a little as he straightens up.

"The stars," I explain. "Now that the *Aurora* is so dark, the stars seem so much…" I pause, trying to think of a way to explain it. "… more real." I'm not sure if this makes sense to him. Each star is so sharp, so clearly defined, that it has become more than simply a little point of light. Like how the moon can sometimes be so incredibly bright. These stars shine with an intensity that steals my breath away.

"Yeah, they do really dazzle now, don't they?" he says.

"Dazzle," I say, turning the word over in my mind. "Yes, that is a really good word for it. It's strange how the stars can be so dazzling even though they're so far away. It's like they're shining straight into my brain."

Wiggs chuckles. Apparently, he finds my description humorous.

We fall silent for a while. I sit, gazing out the viewport, soaking in the beauty of the dazzling stars. A chirp intrudes on my silence. A warning flashes in my suit. It is time to recharge.

"Time to take care of my suit," I say, standing up and stretching.

"I'll come with you," Wiggs replies.

His suit can't be that depleted yet. Wiggs finished charging it just before the visit to Kartak. He must not want to be alone right now. I don't blame him. The darkness is eerie, even when you are sitting right next to someone.

We make our way slowly out the hatchway and down the corridor, to the outer engineering bay. I feel my way along the wall until I find the manual charge unit. Turning on my lamp, I wait for my eyes to adjust to the sudden brightness, and then hook my suit up to the unit. Less than thirty seconds later, I complete the task and switch my lamp off.

Darkness eagerly swallows us once more. It reminds me of riding through the tree in the transparent spheres. A spark of panic flares at the memory. Shuddering, I touch the wall of the engineering bay. It is firm, solid. This, and the steady rhythm of Wiggs's wheezing, helps me subdue the flame of fear.

As my eyes try in vain to pick out anything in the surrounding blackness, I ask, "Do you want to do the honors, or should I?"

"Why don't we take it in shifts," he replies. "I'll go first."

"It's all yours," I say, moving to the side so that Wiggs can access the charger. I hear him fumble around. It takes him a while to find the lever. After that, the bay is filled with his grunting and gasping as he pumps. Barely a minute in, there is a pause. Wiggs must be switching arms.

Smiling, I say, "I guess you're getting your workout for the day."

He manages to strangle out a "No comment" between wheezes.

I take over after about five minutes. It doesn't take long for my right arm to start burning. I keep at it another minute before switching arms. Wiggs and I switch off two more times before my readouts indicate my suit is fully charged. I let go of the lever, pant for a bit to get my breath back, and then check the time. My shoulders sag when I see that we still have almost three hours until supper.

"Should we head to the lounge or the bridge?" I ask, stretching out my arms to gain some relief from the fatigue of pumping the charger.

"Bridge," Wiggs says after a moment. "Our shift doesn't start for another hour, but they might want us on early."

We walk through the dark, silent corridor, bouncing with every step – Marcum is running the gravity generator at 40%. I'm starting to get used to the gait, but it still doesn't feel natural.

"We're here," I say, as my right hand brushes against empty air. Angling slightly to the left, I find the wall of the corridor at the head of the wishbone junction.

Running my hand along the wall beside the hatch, I don't feel the manual control for the door. I feel around some more. Still nothing. Should I turn my lamp on? It would make the search so much quicker. I decide against it. Instead, I run both hands against the wall, searching high and low. Finally, my gloved fingers encounter the control. Fortunately, it only takes a few pumps to get the hatch open. As I enter, my eyes are drawn once again to the fiery stars.

"What's new?" Wiggs asks, as he settles into a seat by the communication station.

Johnson swivels in his seat to face Wiggs. "Marcum has a team working on generator two," he replies. "There is a chance he can get it running. The captain – "

"Would you look at that!" Hollins exclaims, interrupting Johnson. By the faint glow of the control board, I can see that he is pointing out the viewport. I peer out into space, wondering what has caught his attention. I only see stars.

"Look at what?" Johnson asks sharply, his focus entirely back on his piloting.

"There was something…" Hollins begins, but there's no need to finish the statement. Ahead and slightly to starboard, an object materializes in the darkness. It is roughly cubic in shape, and glows slightly. A moment later it disappears, replaced once again by the starry backdrop.

I scan the star field, looking for any sign of the object.

"There it is!" Wiggs exclaims. This time the object is larger and longer – the cube shape that we saw earlier is simply one segment of a much larger object.

"Captain to the bridge!" Johnson calls out. He has switched to a different comm channel, so for us on the bridge, the words are muffled by his helmet.

As I watch, part of the object disappears, but another section materializes farther along. How big is this thing? At first I thought it was roughly four times the size of the *Aurora*, but each new glimpse of it reveals that it is far greater than that.

"What is it?" the captain demands, as he takes a long hopping stride onto the bridge.

"That's what it is," Johnson replies, pointing.

The captain comes to an abrupt halt. His eyes go wide at the sight. "Any communication signal?" he asks.

"Nothing so far," Johnson replies.

And then I hear everyone take a collective breath. Another section of the object has materialized.

And it's only a couple of yards away from the *Aurora*.

CHAPTER 17

The Vessel

"Back us off!" the captain snaps.

Before Johnson has a chance to even move a muscle, the hull in front of us vanishes. So do the stars. Somehow, the *Aurora* is suddenly *inside* an enormous room. Someone gives a yelp. I barely hold back my own cry of surprise.

"Get us out of here!" the captain roars.

"There's no indication of an opening," Johnson replies, his eyes roving over the instrument panel. And of course, with the shape the *Aurora* is in, we couldn't make a quick exit even if we did find a hatchway.

"Something's coming," Hollins says, switching his gaze from the sensors to the viewport.

Craning my neck, it takes me a moment to spot it. At this distance I can't tell what shape it is, or how big.

"Whoa!" Johnson exclaims, lifting his hands away from the control board as if he's been shocked. At the same moment, I feel suddenly heavier. At first I figure this is what has caused Johnson's reaction. But if that's the case, why would he jerk his hands away like that? I look over, puzzled. It doesn't take me long to figure out what has him startled. The control board is fully lit – not the dim lighting of emergency power, but the bright, colorful lighting of a board receiving full power.

Once that mystery is solved, I ponder my weight gain. In the first instant, my mind flashes to the fat planet. Yet my arms are their typical size, and my belly is behaving itself. This is different. The artificial gravity must be back up to its normal level.

"Marcum has fixed the generator," the captain rumbles.

"Not according to the readouts," Johnson says. "They're showing generator output is still dead-lined."

"The readouts must be wrong," the captain says sharply.

"I don't think so," Johnson replies evenly. "Even if Marcum is successful at repairing the generator, it's going to take him a lot longer than this. He's having to do an almost complete rebuild. No, this is something different."

An ominous feeling snakes up my spine. First we find ourselves – interstellar ship and all – inside a cavernous room. Now our systems are receiving power from a mysterious source. I don't know what to make of it.

"Captain, there is a single being outside the hatch," Hollins says.

The captain sits for a moment, evidently thinking the situation over. Abruptly, he pushes himself to his feet. "Somehow I don't think it will do us any good to try and hide in here," he says. "We may as well go greet our welcoming committee."

It's hard to decide how to feel. We are heading out to face the unknown. We've been doing that a lot lately. This is different, though. Before, we visited the various planets willingly. Plus, we usually had a way to make a quick escape. Now we've been swallowed by some enormous vessel, with no apparent way out. If something out there turns out to be hostile, we are trapped.

I stand, a little shakily, and wait for the others to file off the bridge. It would be best to hang near the back. That way, I won't be as noticeable. I hope.

We reach the upper airlock and crowd in. It's apparent that we've developed a herd mentality. No one wants to split off into a second group. Whatever happens, we will face it together.

Johnson is on the other side of the airlock, fiddling with some controls. He is gazing at a monitor, but I can't see what is being displayed. "Computer, give a readout of the environment outside the *Aurora*," he says, as I close the hatch behind me.

"The temperature is seventy-five degrees Fahrenheit," the computer says. "There is an atmosphere of nitrogen-oxygen-carbon dioxide, with other trace gasses. It is breathable. You will not need your spacesuits."

It would be nice to get out of my suit. Three or four days in a spacesuit is a long time. I definitely need a bath. On the other hand, we are facing the unknown. The suit can't stop weapons or anything, but it does offer more protection than regular clothes. Given how strict he has been about quarantine, I'm certain the captain will order us to keep our helmets locked on tight.

To my astonishment, the captain removes his helmet right away. Johnson is next, and then the other adults remove their helmets. Following their lead, I unlatch mine and slip it off.

Surprisingly, the air is warm against my cheek. Just like gravity and the bridge control panels, the environmental systems aboard the *Aurora* have returned to normal. If our generators are in such bad shape, where is the power coming from?

A clank breaks in on my thoughts. The outer hatch slides open, revealing a tunnel sloping downward. The men in front start to disembark. Following right behind Wiggs (figuring he provides the best cover), I step off the *Aurora*, walk to the end of the tunnel, and come to a complete stop.

I don't have words to describe this. I can't see any walls; just an indefinable salmon color at the edge of sight. Yet there must be walls, because I can't see into the distance, either. Have we been transported to a planet without our knowledge? It doesn't *feel* like a planet, but it certainly seems too enormous to be a spaceship. No, a planet doesn't make any sense. It must be some kind of optical illusion. The room isn't really as big as it seems. That's the only explanation I can think of.

The floor is weird, too. There are swirls of color – mostly green and blue. However, they seem to be coming from a great depth, as if I'm walking on a layer of transparent crystal several yards thick.

There is no equipment or furniture in the room that I can see. The only thing occupying the room – besides us, of course – is a single alien waiting about ten feet from the mouth of the tunnel. The alien is wearing a suit of lavender material, including a helmet that completely covers the figure's head. Small lights flash on and off at random across the surface of the suit – these seem to be decorative rather than functional. The alien appears to be fairly humanoid – two arms, two legs, roughly the same profile as a person – but it is shorter and more slender than the adults.

The last aliens we encountered were hostile. These aliens have us at their mercy. How are they going to treat us?

The figure stands silently for quite a while. My heart, already thumping quickly, picks up its pace even more as the tension builds. Should we speak first? How are we ever going to understand each other? As far as I know, none of us thought to bring a graphic pad with the communications program on it.

At last, the figure makes a string of noises. Its voice is smooth and melodious. I'm assuming it is speaking, but the words are gibberish.

"We are humans," the captain says. "My name is Captain Sharta. I'm the leader of the group."

The alien voices another string of gibberish, then turns and starts walking away. We stand in our huddle, looking at each other. What are we supposed to do? Should we stay here? Should we return to the *Aurora*?

After several steps, the alien stops and turns back toward us. It peers at something in its hand, says something, and then turns and continues walking.

"I think it wants us to follow," Dad says.

"I agree," says the captain.

"What about Kartak?" I ask, suddenly remembering the crooked-fingered scientist.

"Hollins, you and Sharden stay with Kartak," the captain says. "The rest of us will go with our guide."

Sharden and Hollins both nod and return to the airlock. The hatch slides shut with a click, sealing them in. The rest of us move even closer together. The alien has stopped once again, and is turned toward us, as if waiting. Squaring my shoulders, I follow the others as we head deeper into the unknown.

———

Once we've closed the gap to within a few feet, the alien turns and leads us onward. Several paces later, my steps falter. One moment, the salmon-colored room seems to stretch on forever. Then in the blink of an eye, our surroundings change completely. We are in a tunnel of swirling turquoise and black. I still can't figure out the walls and floor – they seem to be made out of color rather than solid substance.

After a couple of minutes, the alien turns and walks through what looks like the wall of the tunnel. Everybody stops, unsure what to do. I reach the spot and peer around. This section of tunnel looks like every other section of the tunnel. And yet I can also clearly see our guide through the wall of colors.

The captain sets his shoulders and strides through the colors, followed by Johnson, Marcum, and the scientists. I follow the others hesitantly, wondering what it will feel like to walk through the wall. It turns out, I don't feel anything.

This is more like it.

We are now in a room that actually looks like a room. The walls look solid, the floor looks solid, and there is furniture: a long table laden with food, surrounded by a dozen chairs. My stomach rumbles at the scents wafting up from the steaming platters.

Our guide says something. We look at each other.

"What do you think?" Marcum asks.

"I think we're supposed to sit down," Johnson replies.

The alien makes its intentions clear. Our guide steps to the captain's side, grasps him firmly on the forearm, and leads him to a chair. Captain Sharta pulls the chair out and sits down as if he owns the place.

"What are you waiting for?" he demands, looking over his shoulder at us. "There's plenty of seating."

I choose a seat near the far end of the table from the captain. Thankfully, Wiggs chooses to sit next to me. He will have interesting things to talk about, instead of silly chit-chat.

"Do you think it's safe to eat?" Dad asks, sniffing at the platters of food nearest to him.

"I'm not sure," Johnson says, sounding a little uncertain.

"There's only one way to find out," the captain says, grabbing a dish and scooping food onto his plate.

It is only now, as I watch the captain serving himself, that the oddness of the setup strikes me. This could almost be a dining room on earth: the chairs are the right size and shape (not too surprising, since the alien's body seems fairly similar to ours). What is more surprising are the dishes: they are much fancier than anything I've ever used, but the plates are similar to our plates, the platters are similar to our platters, the utensils are similar to our utensils; everything looks as if it has been made for humans. Have these aliens been studying our world?

The thought is exciting and perplexing. Exciting, because it would mean that finally, we have truly made it back to our own universe. No more false hopes dashed by fat planets. Perplexing, because I have no idea what their intentions are. Why would they be studying us?

On the other hand, if they know so much about us, then they must know the types of food we can eat. This suggests the food should be safe.

With this reassuring thought in mind, I start pulling dishes toward me and scooping food onto my plate.

Everything is delicious. There are meats that are savory, pastries that practically melt in my mouth, and something similar to mashed potatoes. I try not to stuff myself – we've been on food rationing for so long, I don't want to get sick – but it's hard to resist.

None of us speak; we are too busy eating. Our alien guide splits its time between looking at something in its hand, watching us eat, and occasionally uttering something to us. I'm not sure if the alien is encouraging us to eat more, or if it is amazed at how much we are stuffing ourselves, or if its comments are about something else entirely. It's funny, though. Some of the phrases the being uses sound almost familiar. But that doesn't make any sense. I can't be learning the language that fast. It must be a coincidence.

Eventually, I'm stuffed. Even though I've tried not to overeat, my stomach feels like a swollen balloon. The captain is still nibbling on something, but soon even he drops the tidbit and sits back with a heavy sigh.

The alien says something. When nobody moves, our guide strides over to the captain, and again takes him firmly by the arm.

"I guess mealtime is over," the captain rumbles. "Let's see what's up next on today's agenda."

I shove my chair back and rise heavily to my feet. The alien leads us through a wall into another tunnel. After a dozen strides, we walk through the wall on the opposite side.

It's a large bunkroom. Beds line the walls to the left and right. Our guide leads us past the beds, through a doorway at the far end that actually looks like a doorway, and we enter another room. This space has various features. The designs are different from anything I've ever seen, but I'm quite certain I know their functions: bathing stalls, toilets, and sinks. My theories are confirmed when the alien demonstrates how to activate the water in each one.

After we've had a chance to fiddle with the water controls a bit, the alien leads us back into the bunkroom. It grasps the captain's arm and leads him to a bed. The message is clear. It's bedtime.

Our guide says one more thing, which again sounds vaguely familiar, and then leaves the room.

"What do you think?" Dad asks, settling onto a nearby bunk. "Are we being held prisoner like the team was on the fat planet?"

"It doesn't feel that way to me," Wiggs says. "Our host seems to be trying to communicate with us. We've been given a great meal, and now a place to sleep. I think we should take these at face value and assume they're trying to help us."

"How do we know there are more than one of them?" Dad asks. "Don't you think we would have seen others around by now?"

"A vessel this enormous with only one being on it?" Wiggs points out.

"True," Dad admits.

"Plus, there are many reasons why they may be keeping others away," Wiggs continues. "We could be in quarantine. They may be trying to ease our transition. They may have strict social classes, with rules about interactions. I suggest we take it one step at a time, until we have more information."

"I agree," Johnson says. "Let's get some rest, and then see what tomorrow has in store for us."

"I'm going to give one of those bathing stalls a trial run," Wiggs says, levering himself off of a bed.

"I call dibs on one as well," I say, following the big guy.

"Don't use up all of the hot water," Dad calls jovially, as I pass into the bathroom. This makes me smile. With all of their technology, I'm sure the aliens can keep hot water running. Plus, there are six of the bathing stalls. If Dad really wants to bathe, he can take one of the other cubicles.

Inside the cubicle, there is a storage space that appears to be protected from the water. I stuff my spacesuit and shorts onto a shelf and turn on the shower. Streams of pleasantly warm water spray in many crisscrossing jets. There doesn't seem to be any soap. I make do with rubbing my skin down with my hands, and then letting the water pulse against me. It feels great. No more worry about water rationing. I could stand here for hours.

Even so, I don't want to be too wasteful. After letting the water massage me for twenty minutes or more, I shut down the jets and activate the blower. Warm air flows around me, drying my skin quickly. I turn off the air and check my clothes. They are dry. The water from my shower couldn't reach them.

Donning my shorts, I hang my suit over my arm and carry it to the bunkroom. Most of the beds have been claimed. Some of the adults are already lying down. Dad and Johnson are talking quietly. I choose a bed at the far end of the room, set my spacesuit on a shelf, and snuggle down under my covers.

I try to relax, but sleep won't come – things are too strange, and my mind is churning over our situation. Who are these aliens? How advanced is their technology? What does the rest of their ship look like? What are they going to do with us? Will it be possible to communicate with them?

Thoughts continue to buzz through my head. Has Kartak been stabilized? Is he going to make it? Will he blame me for the loss of his legs? And what about the *Aurora*? Will we be able to fix it?

Eventually, I lose track of my thoughts. They drift aimlessly, like the damaged *Aurora*.

CHAPTER 18

The Past is in the Future

Someone is shaking my shoulder. Wishing I was still asleep, I reluctantly open my eyes to see who it is. "Oh, hi Kartak," I mumble, wondering why he is waking me up. It's not like we're on a tight schedule –

I suddenly stiffen and whip my head up. "Kartak! What? How?" I peek over the side of the bed. He has legs! At least, it looks like he has legs.

"They're as good as new," Kartak says, smiling broadly at me. "These guys have the technology to regrow human tissue. It was extremely weird, lying there watching my legs reform. Don't worry," he adds quickly, evidently seeing something in my face. "It didn't hurt even the tiniest bit. Their medical facilities are amazing!"

"Yeah, so is their food," I say, my eyes still fixed on Kartak's legs. My brain just doesn't seem capable of processing this turn of events.

"Yes, I've tasted some of their cuisine," Kartak says, chuckling.

"Do you have any idea who they are, or where they come from?" I ask, still staring dazedly at his new knees, shins, and feet.

"I have no idea," he replies. "They always wore some kind of helmet around me."

"Yeah, our guide did, too." Tearing my gaze away from his legs, I note that Hollins and Sharden are fast asleep on bunks. They must have gotten in sometime during the night.

"Speaking of food, are you ready for some breakfast?" Kartak asks. "One of our hosts is outside the room. I think he's waiting to lead us to the dining room."

"Yep," I say, throwing off my covers. Should I wear my spacesuit? It would probably be more polite than walking around in just a pair of shorts.

Grabbing my suit from the shelf, I quickly pull it on. Wiggs and Dad meander over. From their expressions, I know they've already seen that Kartak is up and about. And like me, they are still in shock at the sight.

"Are you guys finally ready to go get some chow?" Wiggs asks. "I've had to wait hours for you to finish your beauty sleep."

"Yeah, sure," I say, smiling. "You probably woke up five minutes before I did. I'm sure the waiting was just a complete torture for you."

"It was at least ten minutes," Wiggs replies. "And yes, it was torturous."

Shaking my head and laughing, I lead the way into the tunnel outside our room. Sure enough, there is an alien waiting for us. The blinking lights on his suit are different from the ones of our guide yesterday. Is this a different person, or has he simply changed clothes?

He leads us back to the room where we ate dinner. Like last night, the table is laden with all kinds of food. My mouth starts watering at the sight.

Breakfast is every bit as good as supper was. I finish one full plate and another smaller portion. Once again throughout the meal, our host makes comments. The first chance I get, I'll have to go back to the *Aurora*, and grab a graphic pad with the communications program. It looks like we'll be with these aliens for a while. We have to start learning their language, so that we can communicate with our hosts. If nothing else, it will give me something to do.

Kartak and Wiggs dab up the last of their syrup with something like a pancake. Wiggs licks his fingers. Kartak wipes his on a napkin. Our host notes that we're all finished eating. Saying something in his language, he stands and leads us back to the bunkroom.

Hollins and Sharden are still sleeping. Everyone else is lounging or conversing in low tones. My body feels like it could still use another couple of hours of sleep. I remove my spacesuit, lie back on my bunk, and close my eyes.

Just as I'm starting to get drowsy, a voice intrudes on my thoughts. The words are nonsense. It takes my brain a few seconds to realize it's one of the aliens speaking.

Something he says tickles the back of my mind. I try to puzzle it out, turning the sounds over in my brain. Again they seem almost familiar. I'm nagged by the feeling there is something obvious I'm missing, something I should know that just won't quite click in my mind. No matter how much I try, the answer remains elusive.

There is one more clipped statement, and then the alien voice goes away, replaced by the background murmur of hushed conversations.

After a while, I realize I've dozed off. Snatches of dreams whirl around in my mind, making no more sense than the alien language. My mind drifts between sleeping and waking. At times I'm thinking about the alien's language, at other times a few stray words from the scientists drift into my thoughts.

Suddenly, my eyes pop open and I'm wide awake. The answer is so perfectly clear, so perfectly obvious, it's amazing that it has taken so long for one of us to figure it out. Our host was trying to speak Common! That's why it sounds almost familiar.

It's as if the alien has seen Common written, but doesn't know what sounds some of the letters say, so he's made up his own sounds for those letters. He also has a strange accent, which garbles the words even more. I can't understand his speech, but if we have a graphic pad, perhaps we can communicate with him through writing!

Sitting up hastily, I spot Wiggs and Dad whispering on Dad's bunk. "Guys, do you know where any of the aliens are?" I ask, coming over.

"Not at the moment," Dad says.

"What's gotten into you?" Wiggs asks, almost at the same time.

I explain my theory to them. Dad looks excited. Wiggs looks dubious. "Nothing I've heard from them has been intelligible," the big man says.

"If we can get a graphic pad, we can see if I'm right," I say, feeling a little defensive at his reaction.

"Oh, I agree it's worth a shot," Wiggs says. "I just don't think we should get our hopes up too high."

"The next time an alien comes, I'll ask if I can go back to the *Aurora* for a graphic pad," I say, my enthusiasm not at all dampened by Wiggs's skepticism. I am certain I'm right about this.

"Or we can ask if they have something we can use," Wiggs suggests. "If they can understand such a request, it would definitely lend weight to your theory."

"What theory is that?" Sharden asks from over my shoulder, making me jump. I didn't realize he was listening in.

"Sean thinks the aliens are trying to speak to us in Common," Wiggs explains. "Except some of their phonemes are different from what we use."

"That sounds rather farfetched," Sharden growls. "How could they have possibly learned Common?"

"I don't know," I say, shrugging. "Perhaps they've been studying our world."

"That's a cheery thought," Sharden says sourly.

"We're going to try a graphic pad, to see if they can read it," Wiggs says. "I know how unlikely it is, but it's worth a try."

"Nothing will come of it," says Sharden. "But I want to be there when you try. After all, there's nothing else to do in this oversized hotel."

We wait for one of the aliens to show up. Then we wait some more. We try to talk about other things, but the conversation is only half-hearted.

Feeling restless, I get up and pace up and down the room a few times, before coming back to Dad's bed. It has been at least several hours since breakfast. Have the aliens completely forgotten about us? Perhaps they've found something newer and more interesting to gawk at, and have abandoned us.

"How long has it been since breakfast?" I ask, sitting back down beside Wiggs.

"Oh, I would say a little over an hour," Wiggs replies.

"Maybe an hour and a half," Dad concurs.

"What! It's been a lot longer than that," I say

Wiggs chuckles. "The waiting sure makes it feel like a long time, but it hasn't been that long."

"How long do you think it will be before another alien shows up?" I ask, still feeling skeptical about how much time has passed.

"I'm sure they have better things to do than babysit us," Sharden replies.

"It's hard to be sure," Wiggs puts in.

Our conversation lags into silence. Dad starts picking at a seam on his spacesuit. Wiggs twiddles his thumbs. I stand up and start pacing again. Now I know how the tigers in the zoo feel – all the time in the world, and nothing to do.

Perhaps I should go looking for one of the aliens. As far as I know, we haven't been confined to quarters. Sure, I don't know how to navigate through this ship, but I can try to figure it out. After all, what's the worst that can happen? That is, besides getting totally lost. Or bumbling into an alien engine and getting disintegrated. Or finding an alien airlock the hard way.

On second thought, it would be best if I stay right here until one of our hosts comes. I used to be able to wait for hours during a game of Stratagem. This is a splendid opportunity to rediscover that skill.

Finally, my patience pays off. I catch sight of a series of blinking lights. A moment later, one of our hosts steps through the doorway.

By now, everyone has heard my theory. There is a great shuffling as we all head toward the alien. I'm at the back of the crowd. I can't even see our host.

"I suggest Sean do the honors," Wiggs says.

"Go on, Yates," the captain says, stepping back so that I can speak to the alien.

I take a breath. This is the moment of truth.

"Do you have something I can write on?" I ask, using gestures to pretend like I'm writing. Now I feel foolish. This alien isn't going to understand me. How can I get my point across?

Without a word, the alien pulls something out and holds it toward me. It is small enough to fit in my palm. Just before handing it to me, the alien touches something and the device expands. Now it's about a foot wide and half a foot tall.

I take it gingerly. The surface is cool and smooth in my hand. I can't tell what it's made out of. The device is projecting something. It looks like words, but the script is completely unknown to me.

A scan of the device leaves me befuddled. I don't see any controls. How am I going to work this?

Apparently, the alien senses my dilemma. He steps over and taps a couple of places. The writing on the screen changes. Now it's displaying the Common alphabet! I tap several of the letters, and a word forms. It takes a bit of trial and error to figure out how to space my words out. I don't see any way to insert punctuation. Finally, I have a phrase that reads, *my name is sean who are you*

The alien inputs his answer. "*I am the historian.*"

There is a murmur from behind me. I can sense the disbelief. None of them truly believed my theory.

I accept the device back from our host, thinking about what he just told us. He is a historian (or at least, that's the word he came up with to describe himself). Evidently, the historian is the alien with the most time on his hands. Realizing the pun I've just made, I hide a small smile as I start tapping out my new message. *where are we*

The alien reads this, and then taps the controls. After a moment, he turns the projection to face us. Peering at the device, I see the words, "*The past is in the future.*"

"What's that supposed to mean?" Sharden mutters.

Again the alien manipulates the device's controls, then flips the display toward us. Now it reads, "*You are on the future. Your past is being repaired, but you should stay here on the 2,000 year future.*"

I read the statement three times, trying to puzzle it out. It takes a while for me to work through its meaning, and even longer to accept this absolutely absurd explanation.

"He's still speaking nonsense!" Sharden sputters.

"Is he saying what I think he's saying?" Wiggs asks, sounding rather grim.

"I'm afraid so," I reply, still not able to comprehend this turn of events. Surely we must be misinterpreting something. Or is the alien trying to trick us? There doesn't seem to be any reason to, unless he is trying to keep us befuddled. If this is the case, it's certainly working.

The historian inputs something new into the device. It reads, "*How you get here?*"

It's obvious right away that he isn't speaking about how we traveled to this point in space. He knows we came in the *Aurora*. He must be referring to how we've managed to travel into the future.

I look around at all of the adults. "Do one of you want to tell him, or should I?"

"Go for it," Wiggs says.

It's an awkward way to tell a story. I tap a couple of sentences (still without any punctuation), show them to the alien, and then tap some more. I try to include all of the most important details, like when I was writing that play for Mr.

157

Dunberger what feels like ages ago now. And as I pause to think about it, I realize it literally was ages ago. Can we really have traveled two thousand years into the future? Apparently, like so many other things in the rainbow world, time is different. It must skitter past far faster than our own time. Seconds for days, days for years, years for millennia.

After writing about our escape from the fat planet, and then the disaster with the asteroids, I hand the device back to the alien. What does he think of the story? Does he think we're trying to fool him… or that we're insane?

Our host finishes his statement. *"Such place was theorized."* The alien types some more. *"But the scientist was denounced as quack."*

I don't understand the final word. It doesn't make any sense. Perhaps it's a figure of speech? If the scientist was denounced, it must not be a very nice thing.

The alien holds up a new message. *"Here is one for you."*

As I'm pondering the possible meaning of this, another alien comes through the doorway. Without a word, this one takes me gently but firmly by the arm, and leads me away from the others.

"Hey, wait a minute! What are you doing?" I ask.

The figure continues on, as if he hasn't heard me. I crane my head around to look at my companions. Kartak's forehead is furrowed with concern. After a moment, he calls out, "Don't worry, Sean. See what they want."

I catch a final glimpse of them, and then we enter the tunnel and turn right. Feeling some trepidation about being separated from the others, I try to wiggle out of the alien's grip.

The being quickly takes out a device with his left hand, and taps a few inputs. Curious despite myself, I stop fighting to get away. My guide turns the projected words toward me.

"We explore."

CHAPTER 19

Dani

How should I respond? I want to learn more about this place and see what marvels it holds. This might be my best chance to do so. At the same time, I don't want to be separated from the others. Why is this alien only taking me? Why can't Wiggs come along? Perhaps I should suggest this.

Just as I'm about to ask for the communication device, my guide pulls firmly on my arm and we're off again. "Hey, wait a minute," I protest.

My guide ignores me. The tunnel abruptly changes to a large hall. Again, it's hard to tell where the walls are. My surroundings are a uniform gray-white, like a semi-solid mist. We turn right and step into a new tunnel. This one has swirls of orange and black.

It's obvious I have been singled out for this tour. There's no telling why that is. I can either continue to put up a useless fuss, or I can do my best to enjoy it. With some difficulty, I shunt aside my apprehension, and open my mind to the wonders around me.

"I Dani," my guide says suddenly. At least, I think that's what he is saying. This is the first time I've heard him speak. With his odd pronunciation, I'm not entirely sure.

"Is that your name?" I ask. "Dani?"

"My name Dani," the alien replies. The words are still garbled, but understandable… I think.

"I'm Sean. It's good to meet you."

"And you," my guide says.

Nodding, I continue after him in silence. We enter another tunnel. Right away, I spot something weird. Up ahead to my left, there is a slight distortion in the colors of the wall. As we get closer, I realize it's an opening to a room. I'm eager to see what's inside but... should I look? Will it upset our hosts?

It's worth the chance. I want to see everything I possibly can on this vessel. And after all, if they don't want me to see something, they shouldn't leave the door open.

As we draw even with the door, I sneak a peek inside. My first glance is a bit of a letdown. I've seen this kind of room before. There are beds and cabinets... and something that brings me to an abrupt halt. I draw a sharp breath at the sight.

Several of our hosts are standing in the center of the bunkroom, chatting. They are wearing the usual suits festooned with blinking lights. Except their heads are bare.

And they're human.

Not just aliens that look a lot like humans. Not robots that have been modeled after humans. These are real, live, genuine humans.

I quickly turn to Dani. His expressionless face shield stares back at me. Is he angry? Upset? Amused? Will I be separated from the others, now that I know the truth?

My world seems to be spiraling around me. My mind just can't latch on to all of these revelations. It was easier to accept it when I thought we were among aliens with superior technology, and all that talk about being two thousand years in the future was perhaps a misunderstanding. There is no way to cling to such a comfortable delusion now. The facts are clear: we *have* somehow traveled to the future. This is utterly incomprehensible.

Despite the fog that is filling my brain, I suddenly realize that this is why the historian is the one who has been interacting with us. He must be considered the 'expert' on our era. Or perhaps he is studying us, like relics from an archeological dig.

Feeling like I'm about to swoon, I reach out to the wall of the tunnel to steady myself. Dani is still standing beside the doorway, silent and motionless, staring at me. Am I a good specimen for him, providing Dani with information on how ancient humans react to the impossible? Is every reaction I make being dissected and analyzed? And this notion really gets me wondering. Just how much of a lab rat am I? Did they, perhaps, let me see these humans on purpose, just to see how I would respond? The thought is appalling. I have to pull myself together. Act normal, and perhaps one day it will turn from acting into reality.

"More explore," Dani says at last, turning and heading onward.

I clear my throat and give a curt nod. "Right. More explore," I say, forcing the words through my constricted throat. I push off the wall. It takes a few steps to gain my balance. I have to trot to catch up.

Act normal. Right. The only problem is, I have no idea what normal is anymore.

———

Every day after breakfast, Dani comes to pick me up. Three days of exploring the *Mwangaza* (or the *Nebula*, depending on who you ask), and I know I've only seen a small portion of the entire vessel. I don't know how big it is, but I've seen bunkrooms, mess halls, shops, landing bays, sports stadiums, 'farms' (which aren't really farms – there isn't an Earth-equivalent – but it's where they grow food), entertainment halls, data storage rooms, and many rooms that I don't know the function of.

Yesterday was the first day we did something in addition to all of the exploring: we hung out with three of Dani's friends. The conversations were short and chopped and difficult to follow, but I enjoyed them. I'm not sure what they thought of me.

I finish my last piece of toast. Right on cue, Dani enters the dining room. I leave my plate where it is and follow him. We wander through several tunnels, edge along the side of an auditorium, and enter another tunnel. This one looks familiar. I think I know where we're going.

Just a few strides ahead of me, Dani makes a turn. My guess is right. We enter a room I recognize: the bunkroom belonging to Dani's friends that we hung out with yesterday. Only two of the occupants are here. I recognize Qu'arm from the pattern of lights on his suit. I'm not sure whether the other one is Michael or Elias.

"Hi Sean," Qu'arm says.

"Hi Kuwarm," I reply, knowing that I still botch the pronunciation of his name. It's going to take me a while to master the unfamiliar sound.

"Come, try," Qu'arm says, gesturing to something on a rack to my left.

It is a suit of their clothing, complete with blinking lights and face shield. Intrigued, I tentatively touch the sleeve. The fabric is soft and light. "This is for me to wear?" I ask, running my eyes up and down the suit from helmet to soft-soled boots.

"Yes," Dani affirms. "I help."

He takes it off the rack and splits it open down the front, including both legs. I watch with interest – there was no indication of an opening before; I had thought it was one solid piece of material – and I don't see any sign of a fastener.

It takes me a minute to figure out how to slip the suit on, even with Dani's help. Then Dani lines up the two halves of the fabric together, and the suit seals itself up.

I walk around a bit. The suit feels great – even though it's a snug fit, the fabric moves freely and easily and doesn't chafe at all. I jump. My outstretched fingers graze the ceiling of the room. The suit doesn't restrict my movements whatsoever. The boots are extremely light and comfortable. They cushion my landing easily.

Now it's time for the helmet.

I close my eyes as Dani eases it over my head. There is a light pressure as the helmet seals to my suit. My eyes open...

My view has changed completely. Every detail is sharp, every color extremely vivid. Yet nothing looks familiar. It's as if I'm looking at a bizarre alien landscape – all rugged and desolate. Has the suit somehow teleported me somewhere?

Disorientation sets in. When I turn my head even slightly, details flash past as if I'm moving at extreme speed. Vertigo washes over me, almost knocking me off my feet. I don't see Qu'arm where he should be, or the bunk where it should be. What has happened to my eyes? Have we entered yet another bizarre universe? Or is the helmet projecting a holographic landscape – the surface of a moon, or a lifeless planet? Even squinting doesn't help.

I take a step back, trying to spot anything familiar, wishing for an end to the dizziness. It is unbearable. I have to get this visor off!

My fingers probe at the helmet, trying to figure out how to unseal it, how to rip it off my head, when the view suddenly changes. The colors are still vibrant, the details are still crisp, but now things make sense. Qu'arm is right where he should be. So is the bunk.

Puzzled, I look over at Qu'arm. His face suddenly leaps forward. Giving a yelp, I quickly hop back so that he doesn't ram into me. For some reason, his face is far bigger than it should be. It fills my entire field of view, like an enormous hologram. This leaves me utterly confused.

And then I realize what is happening.

The helmet has an automatic zoom feature. When Dani first put it on, I was seeing Qu'arm's face at extreme magnification: pores, creases, imperfections. Then the view switched to normal size, and then moderate magnification. Now it's back to normal size again. There must be a way to control it, but I don't have any idea how. This is something I must learn if I'm going to wear this thing. Otherwise it'll make me nauseous... or drive me loony.

And then it dawns on me. I can see Qu'arm's *face*, even though he is still wearing a helmet. I turn toward Dani. The breath catches in my throat. I feel my eyes bug out and my jaw drop. I stand there and goggle at her. Yes, her.

Dani is a girl.

She appears to be roughly my age. Her hair is dark, her cheeks smooth and white. Her eyes are the deepest, darkest blue I have ever seen. She smiles, flashing a pair of dimples.

I think back on the days we've spent together, the things that I've said, thinking I was talking to an adult guy. I feel my face flush. The deck seems to be sliding out from under my feet...

I quickly shuffle over and collapse onto a bunk. Qu'arm's brown eyes are full of concern. "Okay?" he asks.

I nod, not trusting my voice at the moment. So many thoughts are racing through my head right now. What does Dani think of me? Am I a pet puppy to her? She hasn't treated me like one, but surely she doesn't think of me as a peer – especially after making a fool of myself with all of the things I've said – like the way I spoke about Hilda, when Dani asked about my friends back home.

It's so nerve-racking interacting with them. I haven't been around people my age for so long. And on top of that, now I'm a bumbling idiot from the deep past. It wouldn't surprise me if I have more in common with cavemen than with these teens of the future.

I look up at Dani. The smile is gone from her face. She is staring at me uncertainly. I'm such a fool. I wish I could seep into the deck plates and ooze away. I have to say something. But it's hard with those soft, dark eyes staring at me with concern.

"I'm okay," I mumble, trying to reassure her. "It's just, the helmet is really overwhelming." Which is entirely true, even if it isn't exactly what is causing my anxiety attack right now.

She nods. "The sighting. We used to it. You not."

"Yes, the sighting," I say, glad to have something to talk about. "It zooms in and out at random. I don't know how to control it."

"Mind controls. Take time," Dani replies.

Just then, someone else enters the room. He has brown, curly hair and dark skin. He looks at me curiously.

"Ah, Elias," Qu'arm says. Then he starts talking rapidly in the language they use aboard the *Mwangaza* – completely different from the language the historian tried to use with us. I pick out a word here or there, but most of it is over my head.

Elias smiles at me. "Look good," he says. "Now you are like us."

"Thank you," I say, trying to smile back. I'm sure it's more of a grimace than a smile. I might look a bit more like them now with the suit on, but that is where the similarities end.

At least now I can tell who is who. If this is Elias, then the other person who was here when I entered must be Michael. He has long blond hair, high cheekbones, and watery blue eyes.

Elias turns to Dani. "Almost time," he says in Common.

She nods. "Okay. I take Sean back, then ready." Turning to me, she says, "Come."

By now my mind has almost stopped whirling. My legs should hold me up… I hope.

Rising slowly off the bunk, I turn to the three guys. "Hopefully I will see you later," I say, nodding to each one in turn. And hopefully you will still want to see me, a voice inside my head adds dolefully.

"Yes, tomorrow," Elias says. "You school."

And on that cryptic l note, Dani ushers me out the door.

The tunnel looks different. Even though it still seems to be made of mostly light, I can see the contour of walls, as well as where the doorways to bunkrooms are. Before, I could never see a doorway until I was right in front of it, and even then, the door had to be open. The helmet certainly changes my vision of things.

The change in the look of the tunnel is so intriguing, it's several paces before I remember what Elias said. I hurry up alongside Dani. "School?" I ask her, wondering if I heard him correctly.

She nods vigorously. "We school together," she confirms.

A sense of dread settles in my stomach. Their toddlers probably know more than I do. I don't want to make a complete fool of myself in front of them, especially Dani. How can I possibly keep from looking completely helpless at their academic assignments?

The helmet doesn't allow me to brood on the problem for long, though. The zoom feature keeps kicking in every few feet. Each time this happens, I have to pause and wait for it to decide to return to normal. Dani is very patient with this, even though it makes our journey a lot longer than usual.

Despite the changes in my vision due to the helmet, I recognize most of the places we pass through. There are a lot more people out and about now than there were the first couple of days. They don't seem to pay any special attention to me, even when I'm standing still, waiting for my helmet to behave itself.

We reach the door to our bunkroom. Dani smiles at me. "I go. I come tomorrow." With that promise, she turns and heads back the way we came.

All eyes turn to me when I step into the bunkroom. They gaze at me with idle curiosity, likely wondering who I've come to speak with. I smile, imagining the looks I'm about to see on their faces.

"It's me," I say, striding down the center aisle of the bunkroom.

For a moment, nobody reacts. Slowly, I see some puzzled looks. Then… "Sean?" Kartak asks tentatively, staring as if he is trying to see through my faceplate. The bewilderment on their faces gradually clears, replaced by understanding.

"Yep," I say, stopping next to my dad's bunk.

My smile fades. It's a good thing they can't see my face right now, because I've just realized something.

How do I go to the bathroom in this thing?

CHAPTER 20

Stratagem

My second day of classes is over. Students are slowly filing out. Dani is already at the hatchway. Trying to steel my nerves for what I'm about to ask, I get to my feet and head after her.

My visor still gives me fits. Right now, it seems to be on infra-red mode. All I see are fuzzy, human-shaped images. Dani was just standing up when my visor switched to this mode. I have been following her with my eyes ever since. This is the only reason I know which of the blurred shapes is her. If she exits too soon before me, I will lose track of her.

I pause to let one of the human-shaped blobs exit, and then slip through the hatchway. "Dani," I call, trotting to catch up to her. At least, I think it's her. Sure enough, the fiery image turns toward me.

"I... I was wondering if you wanted to get some ice cream," I say quickly, before I can lose my nerve.

"Yes," she says. "Love to."

My visor switches back to normal, and then immediately zooms in on Dani's face. In a brief moment of clarity, before the magnification becomes too great, I'm able to catch a smile on her face. A tingling excitement spreads through my body. I pause and concentrate my mind. The visor flickers through several different modes, making my head spin. At last, it settles back to normal vision. The smile is still there, making my stomach flutter.

"What is your favorite flavor?" I ask, falling into step beside her.

"I would say –"

I don't hear her finish. I come to an abrupt halt. My visor has gone completely black. I move my head to the left and right, and then up and down, but it doesn't make any difference.

Memories of the dark planet start bubbling to the surface. And the transparent bubbles. And being held prisoner on the fat planet. I feel the muscles in my back tense up. My breath quickens.

After a second or so, there is a faint glimmer at the top of my visor. It moves down an inch, and then disappears. Two thundering heartbeats later, another shimmer appears on the left side of my vision. It floats there for a moment, and vanishes. This is soon replaced by a gleam in the bottom right portion of my visor. It hovers for several heartbeats, and then is gone.

"Something wrong?" Dani asks, sounding concerned.

"My visor. It's cut out. I can't see anything," I explain, forcing the nightmarish memories from my mind. I am on the *Mwangaza*. Dani is here with me. There is nothing to fear.

"Maybe *Uchao* setting," she says. "Look me. See me."

I turn toward her voice, still breathing heavier than normal. The darkness remains before my eyes. What if it isn't something my visor is doing? What if I've gone blind?

I gulp at the thought. If my sight doesn't return… Again, I force myself to calm down. It will be okay. I know Dani is here. I want to see her. I focus my mind on looking at her…

And here she is. My vision has cut back in. Dani's brow is furrowed with concern.

Smiling, I say, "I'm back."

Dani's concern melts away into another smile. "Let's go," she says.

Dani leads me down a series of hallways to a kind of plaza. There is an ice cream stall about half way down on the right. Dani gets two scoops of something I've never heard of.

There are so many options. It's difficult to choose. In the end, I decide to keep it simple. "One scoop of chocolate, and one mint for me," I say.

After we are served, Dani leads me to a corner of the plaza. There is a large rectangle of light on the floor. The air above it seems to shimmer slightly. As soon as we step past the nearest line of light, we start rising. This startles me so much, I start to fall backward. Something catches me and holds me upright. I look down, half curious, half nervous. The floor is dropping away. I seem to be standing in mid-air. We reach a kind of balcony above the shops, and step onto solid floor. "Our table here," Dani says, sitting down.

Crossing over to the chair opposite her, I let out a gasp as a jolt of panic thunders through me. We seem to have stepped right outside the ship. Our table is floating in space. It's just the two of us in a sea of stars. There is nothing supporting my feet. How am I not plunging away from the table, away from Dani?

I hastily put my bowl of ice cream on the table, as my head starts spinning with vertigo. I stumble, and clumsily pull my chair out, hoping to sit down before I collapse. If I miss the chair, I will go falling through the infinite void around us. My hip slides off the seat and I land on my knees, clutching the chair for all I'm worth. My hands are shaking as I pull myself up. I somehow manage to hoist myself onto the chair. All I can do is sit, heaving and quaking.

Dani doesn't seem to notice my discomfort. She has already dipped a spoon into her ice cream. Much to my surprise, she takes a bite – the spoon passes right through her face shield! This is so startling, my fear vanishes. I watch her take another bite. The faceplate doesn't impede the spoon whatsoever.

Taking hold of my spoon, I scoop up some ice cream and... splatter it against my visor. How is she able to make the spoon go through like that?

"Think," she says, chuckling at me. "Use mind."

Think? What am I supposed to be thinking of? I scoop up some more ice cream, and try to imagine the spoon going to my mouth. Again it hits the face plate. I try to move it slowly; I make another attempt, coming in at an angle; I try pausing just before the faceplate. The only thing I accomplish is to get my visor smeared with ice cream. Dani is helpless with laughter.

Finally, I get so distracted by Dani's laughter, that I don't even think about what I'm doing – and the spoon goes right into my mouth! The ice cream is cool and creamy; I have never tasted anything so delicious. I try to ignore the fact that I have a suit on, try to forget about the faceguard. This seems to work. There is still the occasional mishap, but I start to get the hang of eating through the visor.

I think of my dad and the others. What would they think, if they could see me eat like this? Wiggs likes cooking Italian. What would it be like to eat spaghetti through the visor, with the noodles dangling down from the fork, and the sauce spattering everywhere?

"Very good," Dani says, her eyes still twinkling.

"Thanks," I mumble. "I'm glad I could entertain you."

"Ice cream good?" Dani asks.

"Yes, it is very good," I reply, enjoying every bite.

Suddenly, my visor decides to misbehave again. Everything becomes a kaleidoscope: hundreds of pixels of random colors, all mixing and swirling without any clear pattern; I can see movement in the colors, and sometimes there seems to be shapes – but they are so vague, there is no way to make out what they are. I can't see my ice cream, or anything around me. Is the imaging system of my visor broken?

My eyes slip closed for several seconds as I try to clear my head. When I open them again, the kaleidoscope landscape remains. Feeling around on the table, I find the bowl and grasp my spoon. Will the touch of something solid allow my mind to reset the imaging system?

Nothing changes. Blinking doesn't help, either.

Again I close my eyes and think of Dani. I want to see her. I concentrate hard on this thought. She is sitting across the table from me. Her eyes are bright and she is smiling. She has almost finished her ice cream. The picture of her in my mind is crisp and clear. I can do this.

My eyes slowly open. Tension drains from my body. My sight has returned to normal.

She is finished with her ice cream. Chortling, Dani says, "Wash visor."

I nod. "Yes, it needs a bit of attention," I admit, giving a small chuckle of my own.

We get up from the table. After two steps, the starscape vanishes. We are back on the firm floor of the balcony. Dani steps off the edge and starts to descend. It's not easy for me to follow. What if I step off in the wrong spot and plunge down? Or what if the invisible force isn't quick enough to grab me?

Her shoulders are even with the floor of the balcony, and now the top of her head. Steeling my nerves, I take a step into empty air. My left leg starts to sink. I hastily step over with my right leg, but it remains a foot or so higher than my left leg. I descend to the plaza floor like this.

"Bathroom over here," Dani says, pointing to a spot midway along the nearest wall. Her eyes are sparkling with amusement – whether because of my appearance, or because of the way I descended from the balcony, I'm not sure.

"Lead the way."

As I watch melted ice cream trickle down my visor, I have one thought on my mind: I must practice eating through the visor before dining with anyone else.

———

This is a moment for celebration. I have now advanced beyond the toddler stage. I can actually clothe myself! I'm not school-age yet, though. Almost a month of attending classes with Dani, Michael, and Elias has driven home one fact: I have a lot of catching up to do in my studies. Math and science are complicated. Even their 'basic courses' make my head spin.

My dad and the others seem to be feeling increasingly anachronistic. They don't do much mingling with the people from the future. I still spend time with the scientists, especially at night. But large chunks of my days are spent with Dani and her friends: watching shows, playing games, and of course, going to school. And as insane as it sounds, I'm actually starting to enjoy history. It's fun learning about what has happened in the last couple of millennia. In fact, I have just discovered a set of records from my era.

My breath catches when I find an entry that relates to one of my friends. Hoss was a finalist in the World Stratagem Tournament! I feel a twinge of jealousy at this revelation. If I had been back there, I would have been a finalist.

It's so bizarre to think of them as long dead. To me they are still my age. Full of life and energy. A dead weight settles into my stomach as I realize I will never see them again. I will never hear another of Bo's jokes, or Hoss's snorting laughter. Closing down the program with a vigorous jab of my finger, I quickly leave the alcove, knowing I will never return here.

I'll never get to tell Mr. D about my adventures. This is something I've been looking forward to; it has given me something to focus on the past two years, to keep my mind off of the possibility that we might not ever make it back. Now I won't have a chance to tell him about everything. The thought makes me a little sad.

I can't help wondering about something. If gravity, magnetism, and the shields were reversed in the rainbow universe, why wasn't time reversed? Back at the beginning of the trip, this is what I would have longed for: to have a chance to see Mom again, maybe even stop her from dying.

But I realize I'm okay with how things worked out. Yes, I still miss Mom greatly. I don't think that will ever go away. But I'm excited about the future I'm in: the people I'll meet, the things I'll see, the languages I'll learn, the games I'll play...

And speaking of games, they have a variety of games I've tried. The futuristic gaming is weird, but after an adjustment period, I'm starting to get the hang of it. In fact, I had my first victory at Kultak yesterday.

Still, I miss *my* games. In fact, I have decided to teach the youth of the *Mwangaza* that most noble of ancient games, Stratagem.

Movement! Slowly, very slowly, I turn my head so I can look in that direction...

About the Author

A. A. Akibibi is the pen name for Jon Megahan. Jon grew up as a missionary kid in Tanzania, East Africa. He attended an international boarding school, living and interacting with people from many different cultures. He had the great privilege of going on field trips to Mount Kilimanjaro, different wildlife parks, and to the coast to study coral reefs.

Jon currently teaches upper elementary and middle school in rural Minnesota. He enjoys volleyball, disc golf, board games, and Minnesota summers.

Thanks for reading! If you enjoyed this story, please consider telling other people about it. Word of mouth recommendations are important for authors who are just starting out.

For more information, follow Jon on Instagram: aaakibibi